Alba Arango

THE SLEEPWALKING VAMPIRE

A DECODERS MYSTERY

Isab

Published by Sapphire Books
P.O. Box 753842
Las Vegas, NV 89131

Book Cover and Illustrations by Jeanine Henning.

Printed in the United States of America.

For information regarding permission, write to Sapphire Books
P.O. Box 753842. Las Vegas, NV 89136

Library of Congress Control Number: 2018910146

ISBN: 978-1-7323769-9-1 (Paperback)

To the Henderson Writers' Group

Thank you for helping me become a better writer.

CONTENTS

1 THE SLEEPWALKING VAMPIRE

Steve's eyebrows shot up in surprise. "Did you just say your niece is a…vampire?

Matt swallowed his mouthful of chocolate shake in one gulp. "As in, sucks the blood out of people with super sharp fangs, vampire?"

The owner of the diner reclined his tall, dark body back into the chair he had pulled up to the booth, and sighed. "I said, she thinks she's a vampire."

Tyrone Washington was a good friend of the three twelve-year-olds. The kids had just returned to their homes in Beachdale from solving their last case, when they received his phone call saying his niece had a problem he thought the Decoders could help her with. The Decoders was the name of the secret detective team Steve, Matt, and Jenny had created when they started solving mysteries.

Jenny tied her long blonde hair into a bun. "So, why exactly does she think she's a vampire?"

Tyrone drew in a deep breath. "It all started about six months ago. My sister, Abby's mom, would wake up in the middle of the night and find Abby wandering down the hallway, completely asleep. She began taking her to a psychiatrist, hoping to cure her of her sleep walking." He reached over and took a sip from his soda. "For a while, it worked. But then, about three weeks ago, it started happening again. Abby would fall asleep in her bedroom and wake up somewhere else. Once, she woke up outside, lying on a lawn chair near the pool."

Jenny leaned over and stole a French fry off Matt's plate. "Okay, so she's got a sleepwalking problem. What does this have to do with her being a vampire?"

Tyrone leaned in. "Here's the deal. Two nights ago, Abby set up a video camera, you know, to catch herself in the act. The next morning she woke up asleep on the bathroom floor with the window open. The window in her bedroom was open, too."

"Did she get what happened on tape?" Steve asked, completely engrossed in the story.

Tyrone nodded and traced the rim of his cup with his index finger. "When she checked the video the next morning, that's when she saw it."

Matt took the top bun off the burger on his

plate. "Saw what?" He reached for the ketchup bottle.

Tyrone looked around and lowered his voice. "She saw herself get up out of bed, open the bedroom window, then walk into the bathroom. A moment later, a bat flew out of the bathroom, fluttered in circles around the room, and then took off out the bedroom window."

Matt froze. "She turned into a bat?" A massive clump of ketchup splashed on his burger. He frowned and scooped some of it off with a French fry before taking a bite.

Tyrone nodded. "At least, that's what she believes happened."

Steve scrunched his forehead. "That doesn't explain why she woke up asleep in the bathroom."

"Abby thinks when she woke up at night and went into the bathroom, she opened the window in there before her…transformation."

Just then, a waitress waved to Tyrone for help.

He stood. "I'll be right back."

After he left, Steve shook his head. "This theory seems pretty flawed. Why would she need two windows open? Logically, one would be enough. She could easily fly in and out of just her bedroom window."

Matt slurped the last bit of shake from the bottom of his glass. "Dude, the girl's a vampire. I'm pretty sure she doesn't exactly think logically. She's probably got all kinds of crazy thoughts floating through her head."

"Wow," Jenny said as she took a fry off Matt's plate, "sounds like the two of you have a lot in common."

"Very funny." Matt moved his food out of her reach. "But, seriously, this sounds like way out of our league. Maybe Tyrone should call a witchdoctor or something."

Jenny waved her arms wildly in the air. "This is totally in our league." She sounded excited. "Can you imagine if she really is a vampire? It would be like the greatest thing ever."

Matt rolled his eyes. "How is finding a vampire like the greatest thing ever? What are you gonna do when she tries to turn you into one of the undead? I bet she—"

"First of all," Steve interrupted before his two friends began arguing pointlessly, "there are no such things as real vampires. And second, this is Tyrone's niece we're talking about. It's our obligation as his friend to get to the bottom of this and help him out."

Tyrone returned and sat down. "Sorry about that."

Steve sat up straight. "The Decoders would be happy to take your case. When do we start?"

The man looked relieved. "How about tomorrow? I told my sister I had some friends that might be able to help. She doesn't know you're detectives, she just hopes that having some kids Abby's age around will help her with her sleepwalking problem. Abby doesn't really have a lot of friends. They've moved three times in the last two years, so she has a hard time getting close to people."

Matt pushed his brown hair out of his eyes. "Where do they live now?"

Tyrone took a sip of his drink. "In a small town called Timberwood, about half-way between us and Sacramento. By the way, her parents haven't been told about the vampire thing. She only told me because she was hoping I would have some idea of what to do. She's scared her parents are going to put her in a looney house."

Steve turned to his friends. "Do either of you have any pressing matters in the next couple days?"

Matt pushed his empty plate forward and leaned back. "Nope. The only thing I had planned was a trip to the beach. I can put that off for a few days."

Jenny checked the calendar on her cell phone. "I'm free. I just have to double check with my dad and make sure he doesn't need me." Her dad owned a repair shop, and Jenny, who was great at fixing things herself, often helped him out.

"Perfect," Steve said. "Tyrone, we'll make sure it's okay with our parents, then we'll give you a call. Hopefully, by this time tomorrow night, we'll be with your niece, solving this mystery."

The next day, at three-thirty in the afternoon, Steve and his friends walked up the steps to Abby's house.

They rang the doorbell and a beautiful woman in her thirties opened the large, oak door. "Hi, Ty." She reached over and hugged Tyrone. "Thank you so much for coming."

"You know it." He let her go and pointed to the young detectives. "These are the friends I was telling you about. Denise, let me introduce you to Steve Kemp, Matt Peterson, and Jenny Reed. Kids, this is my sister, Denise Samson."

"I'm pleased to meet you, kids." She smiled. "Please, come in."

The group followed her into the house. Mrs. Samson escorted them into the large living room, then left to get Abby.

Steve looked around, admiring the beautiful decorations. The furniture was antique, complimented by sculptures, and portraits hung around the room. He noted that the family was, obviously, pretty well off.

Tyrone's sister returned, leading a girl about a year younger than the three detectives into the room.

Jenny stepped forward. "You must be Abby.

I'm Jenny." She pointed behind her. "That's Matt and that's Steve."

The two boys waved.

"Hi." The girl smiled. "Um, would you guys like a tour?"

They nodded.

The eleven-year-old showed them all around the first floor, then motioned for the kids to follow her upstairs. She led them to the room the boys would be sharing, which had a regular bed and a pull-out couch. The group then followed Abby across the hall, into a room with an identical set up.

She pointed to the sofa. "Jenny's gonna crash here with me. I hope that's okay."

Jenny threw herself on the sofa and sprawled out, giggling. "This is perfect."

Abby looked around, as though making sure no one was listening. She lowered her voice. "I'm really glad you guys are here. I don't know what to do." Her voice sounded shaky. "Uncle Ty said you guys were really good at solving mysteries. You've got to help me stop turning into a vampire."

Steve glanced toward the hallway. "We need to hear everything that has happened so we can take notes. But, not now. Later. I think Tyrone and your parents are waiting for us to join them. As we started up the stairs, I heard your mom mention something about an early dinner being ready soon."

"Dinner?" Matt repeated. "Yes! I'm starving."

Abby headed for the door. "We're having meatloaf and mashed potatoes. I hope you like it."

Matt grinned. "Are you kidding? I love meatloaf."

Jenny stood and followed the others as they made their way down the hallway. "Matt, you love all food. But, you better keep that appetite of yours under control. We don't want to be kicked out of the house before it even starts getting dark outside."

Abby turned back to face them. "No, it's all right. My mom always makes enough food for like fifty people. She's crazy. Sometimes, we end up with leftovers for a whole week."

Jenny laughed. "I don't think that'll be a problem with Matt around."

The boy patted his stomach. "What can I say? I'm a growing kid."

Jenny's blue eye's twinkled. "Yeah, and if you don't watch it, you'll grow right out of those jeans."

Laughing, the kids joined the adults in the dining room. Throughout the meal, Steve tried to take in as much as he could about Abby and her parents. Mrs. Samson was an athletic woman, who looked remarkably like her brother, Tyrone. And, like him, she knew everything and everybody in town. But her face seemed worried. Steve wondered if Abby's sleepwalking was the cause, or if something else was going on.

Abby's dad was tall, darker-skinned than his

wife, more like Steve's own color, with a shaved head, and reminded Steve of Mace Windu from Star Wars. He worked as an engineer and had a wide, cheerful smile.

Then there was Abby. Her hair hung in ringlets and she had her father's dark brown eyes. From what Steve could see, the girl was quiet. She didn't speak much during dinner, and seemed nervous. She played with the food on her plate more than actually eating it.

Matt, on the other hand, had three helpings of meatloaf and praised Mrs. Samson over and over for her amazing cooking skills. The woman beamed from his compliments. Steve smiled. If there was one thing Matt had always been good at, it was making a cook feel like the greatest chef in the world.

Once the meal was over, Tyrone announced he had to get back to the restaurant. He pulled Steve over to the side. "Keep me posted," he said in a hushed voice.

The boy nodded. "I will."

The tall man gave his sister a good-bye hug and left. After closing the door, Mrs. Samson turned to the kids and smiled.

"I'm glad you three will be spending the night. Marcus and I have a benefit to attend and I'm not sure how late we will be. It makes me feel better knowing that Abby won't be alone for too long."

"Mom," Abby said, obviously embarrassed. "I'll be okay."

Mrs. Samson pressed her lips together, then sighed. "It's just that with this sleepwalking thing, I...I just worry about you, Sweetie. Maybe I should call a sitter."

Abby looked horrified. "Mom!"

Steve cleared his throat. "You won't have to worry about her tonight, Mrs. Samson. We're all going to be here with her."

"Yeah," Matt chimed in. "We brought about a hundred movies to watch, and popcorn, and M&M's, and pretzels."

Jenny nodded. "And, once we get tired and go to bed, I'll be sleeping in the same room with her. She'll be fine."

The woman smiled. "Ty did say you three were the most responsible kids he knew."

"May we be excused now?" Abby asked. "I wanna show them the library."

Her mother smiled. "Of course. I'll let you know when we're leaving."

Abby led the kids upstairs into a room lined with bookshelves. The young girl closed the door and motioned for the kids to sit on the various recliners scattered throughout the room.

Steve excused himself for a moment and returned with a notebook and pen. He chose a recliner facing Abby, kicked off his shoes, sat cross-legged, and prepared his notebook for notation. "Okay, Abby, now that we're alone, start at the beginning and tell us everything that's been happening."

She took a deep breath. "One day, about six months ago, I woke up in the middle of the night, and I was lying on the floor in the kitchen. I had no idea how I got there, so I just got up and went back to bed."

Steve scribbled on his paper. "Did something strange happen that day?"

Matt stretched his arms over his head and leaned back in his recliner. "I'd say waking up in the middle of the night in the kitchen counts as strange."

"Really?" Jenny said, a smirk on her face. "I would think that's pretty normal for you."

Matt threw a pillow at her.

"What I meant," Steve said, trying not to laugh, "was, did anything strange happen earlier in the day? Like, maybe at school?"

Abby shook her head. "Nope. Nothing. Then, about a week later, I woke up around midnight, and I was in the living room, lying on the sofa."

"And nothing out of the ordinary happened that day either?"

The girl shook her head again. "When it happened again, about a week later, I finally told my mom."

"What did she say?"

"She said she'd check on me that night. Sure enough, around two in the morning, she found me walking down the hall, completely asleep."

Jenny twirled the tassel hanging from the pillow on her lap. "That's crazy. Did she wake you up?"

"No. She had heard it was dangerous to wake up a sleepwalker, so she just followed me. Mom said it was super creepy, because my eyes were open, but I was totally asleep."

"What happened next?" Steve prompted.

"I went to the dining room and curled down on the floor. Mom woke me up, and I couldn't remember walking there, at all. She and Dad decided I needed to get some help before I hurt myself. That's when they started taking me to Dr. Hollister. He's a psychiatrist."

Matt pulled the lever on his chair to raise the leg rest. "Did it help?"

She shrugged. "I thought so. For a while, the sleepwalking stopped. He came over to the house a few times to make sure I was cured. But the moment I finished our meetings, the problem began again, and worse than before. One time, I woke up outside on a lawn chair next to the pool. That really freaked my parents out. Dr. Hollister figured it was probably just my brain acting out because of the change in routine. He said he'd keep seeing me twice a week, then decrease my sessions slowly to give my body time to get used to the change."

"What are the sessions like?" Steve asked.

Abby bit her lip. "They're always different. Sometimes, we just talk, about random stuff like school or my friends. Sometimes, we do tests."

"Tests?" Matt's face wrinkled, looking like he had just eaten an extra sour Warhead candy. "Ugh. Note to self, no psychologists for me."

Jenny rolled her eyes and threw her pillow at him.

Steve frowned, "First of all, I don't think he's giving her school tests, like math or reading. He's most likely giving her mental tests to help evaluate her brain. And, secondly, it's psychiatrists not psychologists."

Matt shrugged and tossed the pillow up in the air. It landed on the floor next to Jenny. "Tests are tests. It doesn't matter why they're given, they're still tests. And what's the difference between psychiatrists and psychologists. Aren't they the same thing?"

Steve shook his head. "Not exactly. The biggest difference is that psychiatrists go to medical school and can prescribe medicine. The others can't. Has Dr. Hollister given you any medication?"

She nodded. "Yeah, but not to take all the time. He gave me some kind of pill to help me sleep if I get all riled up from sleepwalking. I've only used it a couple times so far, but," she paused for a moment, "after what happened a couple days ago, I'm thinking about using it every night."

"What happened a couple days ago?" Matt asked.

"That's when I found out I'm a vampire."

Matt gulped. "Sorry I asked."

Steve flipped to a new page in his notebook. "Tell us exactly what happened."

She motioned for them to follow her into her bedroom. She and Jenny sat on the bed and the two boys dropped down on the sofa.

"I think it's happened three times. I go to sleep, then wake up on the floor of my bathroom with the window open. After the second time, I decided to film myself so I could show Dr. Hollister what was going on."

She pointed to the dresser on the wall facing her bed. "I set up the video camera over there so I could get a good picture. I hit record and then went to sleep. The next morning, I woke up in the bathroom again. But, when I looked at the video, I...I couldn't believe what was on there."

"Can you describe to us what you saw?" Steve asked.

The girl stood. "I can do better than that. I can show you the tape." She walked over to her dresser, pulled out a video camera from the top drawer, and connected it to the TV. After returning to her bed, she sat down and turned on the television with a remote.

The image on the screen showed her walking back from the dresser and crawling into bed. Abby pushed a button on the remote. "Let me fast-forward to the good part."

The kids watched the monitor. After a few moments, Abby slowed the picture down. "It's coming up."

Steve leaned forward in anticipation. In the video, Abby got up and opened the window next to her bed, then walked into the bathroom.

"Uh, was that it?" Matt asked.

"Just keep watching," Abby said.

The kids continued to stare at the television. Soon, they saw something fly out of the bathroom and circle around the room several times before flying outside through the bedroom window."

Matt jumped up. "Whoa! Was that what I think it was?"

"Can we watch it again?" Steve asked.

Abby rewound the video to the part just before she got out of bed.

Steve moved closer to the TV. There had to be something in there that made sense. Vampires did not exist.

They watched the video a second time. Steve frowned. It was unmistakable. The thing flying out of the bathroom was a bat. How could that be?

2 A SECOND MYSTERY

"Keep watching," Abby said. "I'll fast-forward to the next part."

Matt gulped. "You mean, there's more?"

She nodded. After a few moments, she slowed the tape down. On the screen, the bat returned inside through the bedroom window, flew around the room three times, then disappeared into the bathroom.

Abby clicked off the TV. "The only other thing on the video is me walking out of the bathroom in the morning."

"Did you show this to Dr. Hollister?" Steve asked.

"Are you kidding? There's no way I want him to see that. What if I really am a vampire?"

"Don't you think you should at least tell your parents?" Jenny asked.

She shook her head violently. "They already think there's something wrong with me because of the sleepwalking thing. Can you imagine what they'd think if they found out I was a vampire? They'd probably lock me up in my room forever and send for a witchdoctor or something. Or worse, they'd send me away." She played with the ring on her finger, a look of sadness on her face. "You guys can't tell them, okay?"

They all agreed.

"You promise?" She sounded scared.

Jenny reached over and hugged the girl. "Of course, we promise. We're going to get to the bottom of this. Don't worry."

"Yeah." Matt leaned back on the sofa. "It's why we're here."

A knock interrupted their conversation. The door opened and Mrs. Samson's head appeared. "Excuse me for a moment. Abby, have you seen my sapphire turtle necklace?"

"Nuh-uh. Why?"

Mrs. Samson walked in wearing a floor length blue evening gown. "I planned on wearing it to the benefit tonight. It was out on my dresser, but now it's not there. I thought perhaps you had borrowed it for some reason."

Abby shook her head. "I didn't take it."

Mrs. Samson frowned. "Well, that's odd. I wonder where it could be."

"Could it have fallen on the ground?" Steve suggested.

"I looked on the floor around the dresser and didn't see it. Perhaps I missed it."

"Would you like us to help you search for it?" Steve asked.

She thought for a moment. "Yes. I suppose five sets of eyes are better than one. Come on."

The four kids followed Abby's mom downstairs and into her bedroom. For twenty minutes, nobody spoke as each looked at every inch of carpet on the floor. Finally, Mrs. Samson sighed. "It's no use. It simply isn't here."

"It could be that you put it somewhere else by mistake," Steve suggested, "like inside a jewelry box or something."

She shook her head. "No. I distinctly remember taking it out of the safe last night, and setting it up on the dresser in preparation for the benefit. I can't imagine what could've happened to it."

Steve bit his lip, trying to come up with possible reasons for the necklace's disappearance. "Perhaps it fell on the floor and got sucked up by the vacuum."

Mrs. Samson shook her head again. "The necklace is rather sturdy. It would be impossible for a vacuum to pick it up without making a horrific noise. I'll ask the housekeeper next time she comes in. Maybe she saw it."

"Darling," Mr. Samson's voice broke into their conversation as he walked into the room. "Have you seen my gold cufflinks? The ones with the ship on them?"

She shook her head. "Sorry, Dear, I haven't."

"Oh, well. I guess I'll wear the ones with the alligators." He grinned and disappeared into the walk-in closet.

"Dad's cufflinks are gone, too?" Abby said. "Isn't that weird?"

"Hm." Mrs. Samson glanced at her watch. "Janice probably put them all someplace else. Listen, kids, I have to finish getting ready. Are you sure you'll be okay here by yourselves?"

Abby rolled her eyes. "For the millionth time, Mom, we'll be fine."

Mrs. Samson kissed her daughter on top of her head and ushered the kids out of the room, closing the bedroom door behind them.

Steve glanced back as they walked up the stairs. "Does anyone else think it's strange that both the necklace and the cufflinks are missing?"

"Not really." Matt walked into the library and stretched out on the floor. "My mom loses stuff all the time. She'll swear she left it in one place, then we'll find it someplace else. Usually, she's like, 'oh, yeah, I forgot I put it there'."

Steve sat on one of the recliners. "Still, these are expensive items to simply misplace."

Jenny sat cross-legged on the ground next to Matt. "What about the maid? What if she's been stealing stuff and pawning it on the side?"

Abby put her hand up. "Hold on. Janice is no thief. She's been our maid since before I was born. I think she even worked for my dad before he met my mom. She's like super sweet."

Matt pulled a bag of M&M's out of his pocket. "In that case, she probably saw those things lying around and decided to put them someplace safe so they wouldn't get stolen." He ripped the bag open and chocolate candies went flying all over the floor.

Abby nodded. "I'll ask her next time she's here."

"Speaking of someplace safe," Jenny said as she began helping her friend pick up the candy pieces from the floor. "What's the plan for tonight?"

Steve took the small wastebasket next to him and handed it to Matt. "There's really nothing for us to do until bedtime, so I suggest we dig into that pile of movies we brought and find one to watch. When bedtime gets closer, we'll finalize a plan."

Everyone agreed and relocated to a room the Samsons had converted into a home theater. The kids rummaged through the stack of DVDs and found two old Disney cartoons they hadn't seen in a while.

Although the movies were some of his

favorites, Steve was only half-way watching. Something about the disappearing jewelry bothered him. Both items were things they had planned on wearing this evening. Mrs. Samson mentioned taking the necklace out of the safe last night. If it was a thief, they chose a lousy target. This house had so many valuable artifacts all around it. Why choose something that would be obvious to the owners it was missing?

At around eleven o'clock, the group decided to turn in. Jenny said good-night to the boys and promised to text them if anything happened. She put on her pajamas and looked at Abby's bed. What if the girl got up and changed into a vampire and Jenny slept through it? She glanced around the room and saw something that gave her an idea. "Hey, Abby?" She pointed to the top of a bookcase in the room. "Is that a roll up piano I see up there?"

"Yeah, but I don't ever really use it."

"Does it work?"

She nodded. "The keys are kinda hard to get used to, but it plays okay."

Jenny thought a moment. "Would you be okay with putting it on the floor next to your bed?"

Abby frowned. "Why?"

"That way, if you get up in the middle of the night to change into a vampire, you'll step on it and wake me up."

Abby's eyes lit up. "That's such a cool idea. Let's do it!"

She jumped up, grabbed the chair from her desk to use as a stepping stool, and reached up to get the piano. Once in place, Abby stepped on it to make sure it made noise. A loud set of notes emerged from the small speakers. "It works!"

Jenny clapped her hands. "Perfect! Now, if you get up at night, I'll hear you."

Abby grinned and crawled into bed. "That makes me feel a whole lot better."

The two girls said good-night and turned off the lights. Jenny stared at the ceiling for a while, thinking about what she would do if her new friend did indeed turn into a vampire and chased her around the room. Abby was smaller than her so Jenny was pretty sure she could take her down, but vampires were supposed to have superhuman strength. And if the girl turned into a bat, there'd be no way to catch her. She closed her eyes and drifted to sleep, wondering if her parents would recognize her as a vampire.

The sound of music notes filled the air. Jenny opened her eyes in surprise and hurried to turn on the light. Abby was walking toward the bathroom.

Jenny hopped out of bed. "Abby!"

No response.

"Abby," she said louder. She walked up behind her and touched her shoulder.

The girl turned around. Her eyes narrowed and she hissed.

"Abby, it's me. Jenny. You've got to wake up."

The young girl hissed again, only this time, she showed her teeth.

Jenny gulped. Abby had fangs!

The vampire girl turned and walked into the bathroom, closing the door behind her.

Jenny ran to the nightstand, grabbed her phone and dialed Steve's cell.

"Hello?" A sleepy voice answered the phone.

"Steve, it's Jenny. Wake up Matt right now and get over here. Abby just turned into a vampire!"

Within a minute, Steve and Matt were at Jenny's side.

"What exactly happened?" Steve asked.

Jenny related everything from the roll up piano idea to Abby's hissing and vampire fangs.

Matt yawned and stretched his arms over his head. "Are you sure you didn't imagine that? I mean, you were just asleep. You probably just dreamed the whole vampire thing."

Jenny crossed her arms and narrowed her eyes. "I know what I saw. Abby hissed at me and she had fangs. There's no way I would make that up."

"Okay," Steve said calmly, "let's see if we can get her to come out of the bathroom. I'm sure there's a logical explanation for all of this." He walked over to the bathroom door and knocked. "Abby?" He knocked again. "Abby? It's Steve. Open up." He leaned his ear up against the door.

No response.

"We just want to help. Can you open the door? Please?"

Steve turned the door handle. It moved. He stood back. "Jenny, you should be the one who walks in."

Jenny nodded and stepped forward. She turned the handle and slowly pushed the door open. "Abby?"

Suddenly a giant bat flew over her and into the bedroom. Jenny squealed and waved her arms wildly over her head to keep the bat from touching her. Matt ducked and covered his head with his arms. Steve also knelt down, but kept his eyes on the bat.

The creature flew a couple times around the room then flew out the bedroom window.

Matt stood slowly. "Holy Smokes! She really did turn into a bat."

Steve turned and walked into the bathroom. It was empty. The bathroom window was closed. "I...I don't believe it."

3 A STAKEOUT

Steve stared in disbelief. Matt slapped him on the back as he joined him in the bathroom. "Believe it, dude. Abby is a one-hundred percent, total vampire."

"But…but, that is a scientific impossibility," Steve stammered. "There are no such things as vampires."

"Yeah, well, tell that to Abby," Matt said. "You know, when she flies back here and tries to turn us into members of her vampire coven."

Steve shook his head to clear it, then took a deep breath "One thing at a time. We need to locate Abby. Come on, let's find out where this 'bat' went."

The three kids changed into regular clothes, grabbed flashlights from their mystery backpacks, and snuck down the stairs, trying not to wake up the parents. They found their way to the back door, unlocked it, and quietly went outside.

Flashlights on, they split up to explore the entire yard. The Samsons owned about five acres, so the search was not going to be a quick one. Steve focused on the area that led to the pool. Earlier, Abby said she woke up once on a lawn chair near there. Perhaps that was where she went now. Suddenly, a bat flew over him, high in the sky. It circled around the backyard a couple times, then swooped down and disappeared somewhere ahead of him.

Steve resumed his walk toward the pool. What was that bat doing? There had to be some kind of explanation that tied the bat to Abby's disappearance. But what?

"Did you see that?" Matt's voice cut into his thoughts.

Steve whirled around and waited for Matt to catch up to him. "Yeah. It looked like the bat disappeared somewhere up there."

"Hey, guys, hold up." Jenny ran up to them. "Did you see the bat flying around?"

Matt nodded. "Yep. That's what we're gonna go check out now."

"Do you think it was Abby?" Jenny asked.

"Who else would it be?" Matt said. "I mean, unless there's like a whole swarm of vampires in the area. Hey, maybe Abby's parents are vampires, too, and they didn't want Abby to know until she was old enough. But now she's turning into one of them and they don't know because she hasn't told anybody. Maybe—"

"Matt," Steve interrupted. "Abby is not a vampire. Her parents are not vampires. There is no 'swarm' of vampires."

"Then how do you explain what we saw?"

"I don't know," Steve admitted. "But there has to be a logical explanation."

Jenny stopped. "I don't mean to interrupt you, but, look!" She pointed to a lawn chair near the pool. Abby lay curled up on it, asleep.

"Yep," Matt said. "That's right about the place where the bat swooped down and disappeared. And now we know why. It turned back into its human self and fell asleep."

The three kids walked up to the sleeping girl. Jenny knelt down and gently shook her.

Abby slowly woke up and squinted up at the trio. "What's going on?" She yawned. "Did something happen?" She looked around and her eyes grew wide. "How did I get out here? Did it happen again?"

Steve glanced over his shoulder. "Let's get back inside before someone notices we're gone. We can discuss what happened once we're upstairs."

They all agreed and snuck carefully back into the house and up the stairs. They waited in Abby's room while Steve went to get his notebook. He returned and flipped to a new page.

"Okay, Abby, tell us everything you remember."

Her forehead scrunched and she closed her eyes. After a moment, she opened them and looked at Steve "I was talking to Jenny about the roll up piano being a good idea. We said good-night and then…then…I guess I fell asleep. The next thing I remember is Jenny shaking me to wake up and I was outside. How did I get there? Did you guys see me sleepwalking?"

"Not exactly *walking*," Matt said.

"Huh?"

"One thing at a time," Steve said. "Jenny, your turn. Tell us exactly what you remember."

Jenny recanted her experience. When she got to the part of the young girl hissing at her and exposing her fangs, Abby reached for her own mouth and felt her teeth. Jenny finished her story with their search for missing girl and how she saw the flying bat outside, started to follow it, met up with the boys, and then found Abby asleep by the pool.

Steve flipped the page in his notebook. "Now, Matt, your turn."

Matt told his story of being awakened by Steve, going into Abby's room, seeing the flying bat, and going outside. Then, as he searched the outside, he saw the flying bat and the rest of his story was just like Jenny's.

Steve nodded. "And my story is the same as Matt's. So there are a few things we can say for certain. One, Abby got up and went into the bathroom."

"After hissing at Jenny," Matt interjected.

"Yes," Steve continued. "Next, the three of us opened the bathroom door and saw a bat fly out and into the bedroom. The bat circled around the room a couple of times and flew out the bedroom window."

The others nodded.

"Next, we walked into the bathroom and Abby was gone. She was not in the bathroom, nor in the bedroom."

"And, the bathroom window was closed," Jenny added.

Steve nodded. "Next, we all went outside where the three of us saw a bat, not necessarily the same bat that was in the bedroom, fly around outside, then disappear somewhere in the yard. Next, we followed the flight pattern we believed the bat took before it disappeared and found Abby asleep near the pool. Does that sum up everything we know for certain?"

"That and the fact that Abby's a vampire," Matt said.

"Matt!" Jenny scolded. "We don't know that for sure. You're gonna scare her."

"I didn't say she was a crazy, blood-sucking vampire," Matt said. "Maybe she's a super nice vampire."

Jenny frowned. "Matt, you seriously need to stop talking now."

"No, he's right." Abby shook her head. "I am totally a vampire. It's what I was afraid of." She looked scared. "What am I gonna do?"

"First of all," Steve said soothingly, "there are no such things as vampires." He cast a disapproving look at Matt. "We're going to figure out what's really going on."

"How?" She asked, her voice nervous.

"It's what we do." Jenny smiled. "We're detectives."

Abby gave a half-smile. "Do you guys really think you can help me?"

Steve nodded vigorously. "Absolutely. The Decoders have never lost a case. Now, I suggest we all get some sleep and try to come up with a plan in the morning."

They all agreed and went back into their bedrooms. Matt collapsed on his bed. "Dude, do you really think there's a logical explanation for this?"

"Yes," Steve said and lay down. "Abby is a vampire."

Matt jumped up. "What? I thought you said there was no such things as vampires."

Steve roared with laughter. "That was too easy."

Matt threw a pillow at him. "Not cool, dude. Not cool."

After saying over and over that he was just joking and he really didn't believe in vampires, Steve finally got Matt to go to sleep. But he couldn't fall asleep himself. There really was no logical explanation. Abby went into the bathroom and a bat came out. A bat flew over the backyard and landed near the pool and that's where they found Abby. The truth was, the only logical explanation was that Abby was indeed a vampire.

The next morning, Steve and his friends met Mrs. Samson down in the dining room for breakfast. She had made omelets for everyone.

Matt grinned as he sat down. "This is great, Mrs. Samson. I love omelets."

"I'm glad to hear that. Listen, do you kids have any plans for the day?"

They all shook their heads.

"I'm meeting an old college friend of mine for lunch. The restaurant is right down the street from the mall. If you like, I could drop you all off at the mall for a couple of hours, then pick you up when I'm done with my lunch date."

Both Jenny and Abby said yes so fast that the boys didn't even get a chance to object. Steve grunted. It wasn't like there was anything they could do about their case until the evening, but spending an afternoon at the mall did not sound like fun, at all. He was pretty sure Matt would agree with him.

"They have a huge food court," Mrs. Samson added.

Matt's eyes lit up and Steve sighed. Now there was no way he could get out of it.

A couple hours later, the group prepared to leave the house. As they walked out the front door, Mrs. Samson stopped short, looking at her right hand. "I forgot my ring. Hold on a moment, kids. I'll be right back." She disappeared into the house.

Matt plopped down on one of the front porch chairs. Jenny and Abby sat on the swing. Steve remained standing.

Matt leaned forward to study a trail of ants on the ground. "I wonder what kind of food places they have."

"Who cares?" Jenny asked. "I wanna know what kind of clothes stores they have."

Abby laughed. "It's a really big mall. They've got all kinds of stuff there. They've got tons of clothes stores and shoe stores. Their food court is ginormous. And they have this super big bookstore which is pretty cool."

Steve perked up. "They have a bookstore?"

She nodded. "It's huge. You're gonna love it."

Steve smiled. That was a reason to go to the mall.

Just then, Mrs. Samson came out, a concerned look on her face.

"Is something wrong, Mom?" Abby asked, obviously noticing the same thing.

The woman began walking toward her car. "My college ring is missing. I wear it every time I meet with Samantha."

"Are you sure you didn't misplace it?" Steve asked. "When was the last time you wore it?"

She shook her head. "I keep it in a special jewelry case on my dresser along with my diamond earrings."

"So, the earrings are gone, too?" Steve asked.

"No." She sighed and smiled. "What am I thinking? Why would a thief steal my college ring and not my diamond earrings which are worth twenty times more? You're right. I must've simply misplaced it."

Steve frowned as they climbed into the car. Mrs. Samson mentioned the word 'thief.' Was she also thinking someone was stealing her jewelry?

Abby's mom dropped them off at the mall, promising to pick them up in two hours. Once inside, the kids split up. Steve wandered into the bookstore and began scanning the shelves. He soon came across the section of the store with graphic novels. Although Steve was not much into the genre, he did like looking at the covers. One particular book caught his attention. It showed a young girl vampire.

Curiosity got the better of him. He picked up the novel and skimmed through it. According to the story, the girl changed only at night, and her own parents didn't even know she was a vampire. During the day, she was a typical teenager. Then at night, she fought crime and helped out the police. Steve almost put the book back when a passage near the end caught his attention.

She couldn't help it. Jewelry was her only weakness.

He read it again then closed the book and put it back on the shelf. He shook his head and told himself to stop being ridiculous. There were no such things as vampires. Abby was not a vampire, and she was not stealing her parents' jewelry.

The kids met up just before the appointed time. Matt went on and on about the variety in the food court and how he sampled food from about a dozen different places. Jenny showed off the new pair of boots she bought and the amazing sale price she paid. Then she went on to talk about each of the three shirts she bought, all on clearance.

Matt popped his last piece of caramel corn into his mouth, wadded up the wrapper, and threw it into the nearby trash can. "What'd you end up doing, dude?"

Steve shrugged. "I just hung out in the bookstore."

"Find anything interesting?" Jenny asked.

He shook his head. No way was he telling them about the graphic novel or the vampire girl that had a weakness for jewelry. Matt would be on his cell phone in a flash searching the internet for a witchdoctor for Abby.

Mrs. Samson pulled up and the group got in the car to head back to Abby's home. Once they arrived, Abby's mom disappeared into her bedroom and the girls ran upstairs to try on their purchases one more time. Matt yawned and announced he was going to take a quick nap and headed upstairs.

Steve decided to take the alone time to get a good feel for the layout of the house. If there was a thief, he or she was getting in the house, somehow. He chose to start his investigation in the living room near a big window that faced the front yard. A beautiful antique sofa, burgundy with gold trim, rested in front of the window graced with large, swoopy drapes on each side.

The detective pushed one of the drapes to the side to get a look at the window. It was locked from the inside and had a small wooden stick nestled in the grooves to keep anyone from opening the window without removing the stick. No way could a burglar sneak inside this way.

He continued his exploration of the house by

moving into the dining room. Ten chairs were positioned around a large table with a crystal chandelier hanging above its center. The small window against the wall faced the side of the house. After careful examination, Steve confirmed that it could not be opened.

The next room was the large family room. It faced the backyard and had several windows, each of which had miniblinds covering them. He walked up to the first and raised the blinds half-way. Like the window in the living room, this one also locked and had a small wooden stick preventing anyone from opening it from the outside. A similar check of the other windows revealed the same.

The only room on the bottom floor left to check was the Samsons' bedroom, and Steve was not about to go in there. At least, not while either of the parents were home. He walked into the downstairs guest bathroom to wash his hands. As he dried them on the towel, he heard Mrs. Samson's voice.

"I don't know what to do," she said.

A pause made Steve believe she was on the phone. He was just about to walk out of the bathroom when he heard her speak again. This time, her conversation caught his attention.

"No, we aren't going to call the police just yet," she said. "Marcus and I want to see if we can get to the bottom of this first. What if it's one of our friends? We've had so many guests in the last few months. Tonight, we're going to thoroughly check all our jewelry and see if any more items are missing." She paused. "So far, it's my graduation ring, my sapphire turtle necklace, my jade necklace, my sapphire pendant, and Marcus' gold cufflinks. What? No problem. I'll call you tomorrow. Bye."

Steve closed the door to the bathroom and ran water in the sink. He didn't want Abby's mom to think he had been eavesdropping. His mind processed everything she had said. Several jewelry pieces had gone missing. And several guests had stayed at the house recently, so any one of them could've seen where she kept her jewelry and returned to steal it.

He frowned. But Mrs. Samson's sapphire necklace went missing yesterday. The only guests in the house were the Decoders. Something else was going on, but what?

Later that evening, he told Matt and Jenny what he had overheard.

"Do you think we should tell Abby?" Jenny said.

Steve shook his head. "Not yet. She's got enough to worry about without thinking there's a thief stealing things out of her house. It might freak her out."

"It's freaking me out," Matt said. "And, I don't even live here. How the heck is this guy getting in and out of here?"

Steve shrugged. "I don't know, but here comes Abby. Let's talk about this later."

"Mom told me to tell you guys that dinner's ready."

Matt grinned. "Greatest words on the planet."

They followed the girl downstairs to the dining room. There were several platters on the table filled with baked chicken, mashed potatoes, corn, and fresh biscuits. The kids ate heartily, and Matt declared Mrs. Samson the world's greatest cook. She smiled at the compliment, but Steve could tell both the adults were distracted. He wondered if they had discovered any additional missing jewelry items.

After dinner, Abby's parents asked her to join them in the family room to Skype with her grandparents. The three detectives went into the theater.

Jenny leaned back on the sofa and used the remote to turn on the TV.

Matt plopped down on a recliner. "So, what's the plan?"

Steve sat on the sofa next to Jenny. "We have to figure out what to do about Abby."

"You mean, we have to figure out how to keep her from turning back into a vampire bat." Matt pulled out the leg extension of the recliner and leaned back so he was almost lying down.

Steve frowned. "What we need is a way to

watch her at all times, so we can figure out what's going on."

Matt gave a short laugh. "It's really not that complicated. She turns into a bat and flies out the window. We saw it on the video tape, and then we saw it for ourselves. With our own eyeballs."

"Correction." Steve held up his hand. "We saw Abby walk into the bathroom and a bat fly out. And as you recall, it was the same thing on the tape. We have no evidence that Abby and the bat are the same being."

"Yeah," Jenny said slowly, "but when we went into the bathroom, Abby was gone. If she didn't turn into the bat, then where did she go?"

"That's what we've got to figure out. How can we make it so Abby never leaves our sight?"

Jenny shook her head. "We can't. Once she goes into the bathroom, we lose her. It's not like we can exactly follow her in there."

Steve thought for a moment. "No," he said finally, "but we could do a stake out."

"What do you mean?" Matt asked.

"I think we should take turns watching Abby. As soon as she gets up to sleepwalk, we should track her every move. Then—"

"Hold up," Matt interrupted. "You want us to wait for her to sleepwalk and follow her? What if she turns into a bat and flies out of the house again? How are we supposed to watch her then?"

Steve bit his lip. "None of us has actually seen Abby turn into a bat. We saw her go into the bathroom and a bat come out."

Jenny shrugged. "That's true, but Abby also disappeared from the bathroom. We didn't see her again until we went outside."

Steve nodded. "Good point. Matt, I'm stationing you outside."

"What?"

"Both the time stamp of the video tape and the time of our encounter with the bat were around one o'clock. I figure we'll wait till around midnight. Then Jenny can let me into the girls' room and the two of us will wait for Abby to begin her sleepwalking."

"What about me?" Matt asked. "What am I gonna be doing?"

Steve smiled. "You'll be waiting outside, just in case."

"Great. So I get her once she's already turned into the crazy bat looking for blood to feast on."

Steve rolled his eyes. "Abby is not a bat. But she is getting out of the house somehow. If she's crawling out her window while she's sleepwalking, then, Matt, you'll see her and be able to make sure she doesn't fall and hurt herself." He scratched his chin. "Something is going on, and we need to figure out what."

"Shh," Jenny whispered. "Here she comes."

The kids greeted their friend and put in a movie for them all to watch.

At around eleven o'clock, the group said good-night and separated. Jenny turned off the light and lay in bed, waiting. At midnight, she snuck over to the bedroom door and opened it.

Steve entered and shut the door silently behind him.

"Anything going on?" he whispered.

"Nope. Abby's asleep. Is Matt outside?"

"Yeah. And grumpy, might I add."

Jenny chuckled. "I wish I could see his face right now. He's probably looking up at the window, cursing at us."

Steve pointed to the dresser. "Let's sit on the floor over there. We'll have a good view of Abby if she gets up, and we'll be out of her way in case she does."

Jenny agreed and the two friends sat down in front of the dresser to wait.

A few minutes after one, Steve heard a very faint ringing, like that of an old-fashioned telephone. It was so faint, it sounded like it came from very far away. Then it stopped.

"Did you hear that?" he whispered.

"Yeah. What was it?"

He shrugged. "I don't know."

At that moment, Abby sat up, pushed the covers off herself, and slid out of bed.

The detectives stood, prepared to follow her. Abby hovered over the nightstand for a moment, her back to them. Steve thought she was getting ready to turn on the light and pondered how awkward it would be having to explain what he was doing in there. But soon, she turned, opened the window next to her bed, and headed for the bathroom.

"Come on." Steve moved slowly toward the girl. Jenny followed closely behind him.

Suddenly, Abby turned around, faced them, and hissed, her open mouth revealing two large fangs. Vampire fangs.

Steve and Jenny instinctively backed up. Abby continued hissing until they had backed all the way to the dresser. She then turned and walked into the bathroom, closing the door behind her.

4 A BAD SIGN

Steve stared at the bathroom door.

"You saw that, right?" Jenny said, her voice shaky. "I'm not crazy."

Steve shook his head. "I saw it, but I don't believe it. Come on, we've got to get into that bathroom."

He ran up and tried turning the doorknob. Locked. "Abby? It's Steve." He knocked. "Open up."

No answer. He tried the handle again. "We've got to get in there, without breaking down the door, preferably."

Jenny bent down to examine the doorknob. "Hold on. This is one of those child safe locks. All we need is a pin. I've got one in my backpack." As Steve reached over to turn on the ceiling light, she ran to her backpack and dumped everything on the bed. "Here!" She held up a large paperclip. "This'll do it."

Jenny returned to Steve's side, opened the paperclip so it had a long side, and stuck it into the key hole.

Outside, Matt had spent the last hour grumbling to himself about always getting the dangerous missions. And cold. He had already zipped up his jacket and covered his head with the hood. After a while, he pulled a small lotion bottle out of his pocket. Jenny had given it to him to hold the other night at the diner, and he'd forgotten about it. Matt popped the lid and put some on his hands. It smelled good. He poured out a little more and rubbed it on his face. After stuffing it back in his pocket, he glanced down at his watch. One o'clock. He looked up, waiting to see if anything happened.

Soon, Abby's bedroom window opened. He couldn't get a clear view of who had opened it, but he saw a figure moving inside. Then he heard a noise from the ground near his feet. It was weird, like the sound of a bunch of pebbles hitting the floor. Seeing nothing unusual around him, he turned his attention back up to the house. Abby's bathroom window was now open, as well.

A rustling in the trees behind him distracted Matt. He whirled around, shining his flashlight into the shrubbery. Everything appeared normal. As he turned back, something in the sky caught his eye. A giant bat was flying directly at him! Matt put his hands up to protect his face. As the winged creature flew around his head, Matt gave a shout and began waving his hands around, trying to get it to fly away. When it refused to leave and continued flying around him, Matt took off running, flapping his arms wildly in the air, knowing he was about to become a vampire.

Steve watched as Jenny knelt on the ground, struggling with the paperclip. Finally, they heard a click in the key hole. She turned the handle and peeked in. "Abby?" No response.

She opened the door wider. The bathroom was empty and the window wide open. Both kids ran to look outside. No sign of Abby or Matt.

"We've got to get down there," Steve said.

The two kids rushed down the stairs as quietly as they could, hoping to not wake up Abby's parents. They slid open the back door, ran outside, and softly called out Abby and Matt's names. Soon, they noticed movement on the path toward the pool. They hurried over and found Matt walking rapidly toward them.

"What happened?" Jenny asked, a look of concern on her face.

Matt bent over, gasping for air. "I was attacked."

"What?" Steve and Jenny said simultaneously.

He stood straight and tried to relax his breathing. "A bat flew down from Abby's room and attacked me." He paused to catch his breath. "Please tell me Abby's still up there and it wasn't her that just chased me around the backyard, trying to suck all the blood out of my body."

Jenny shook her head. "She's not there. She disappeared, just like last time."

Matt shuddered. "Well, she didn't exactly disappear. She turned into a bat. I told you she was a vampire."

"What happened to the bat?" Steve asked.

Matt pointed behind him. "I ran that way, trying to save myself from becoming one of the undead. She followed me for a while, then finally flew away. I don't know where she went."

Steve started walking in the direction of the pool. "Come on. Our priority now is finding Abby."

As they neared the swimming pool, they saw her…asleep on the lawn chair, just like last time.

"What are we gonna do?" Jenny asked. "Do you think we should tell her parents?"

"One thing at a time," Steve said. "Let's get Abby back upstairs. Once she gets to sleep, we'll regroup and recount everything we saw. Perhaps we can learn something new. For now, let's keep quiet on the whole bat thing."

Jenny looked distressed. "What are we gonna

tell Abby? She's gonna want to know what happened."

Steve thought for a moment. "Perhaps we won't have to tell her anything. Matt, do you think you could carry Abby all the way upstairs?"

Matt shrugged. "I think so. But don't you think she'll wake up?"

"I don't know, but it's worth a shot. And if she does wake up, we'll tell her we fell asleep, and when we woke up, she was gone and we found her out here."

Matt picked up Abby as gently as he could. The young girl stirred but did not wake up. They crept into the house, placed the sleeping girl into her bed, then relocated to the boys' room.

Jenny and Steve sat on the couch and Matt plopped down on the bed. Steve pulled out his notebook and pen. "Okay, Matt, let's start with you. I want you to take your time and tell us, step by step, everything that happened."

Matt recanted his tale, careful not to leave anything out. When he got to the part about the bat flying toward him, Steve stopped him.

"Hold on a moment. Go back. You said the window to the bathroom was open *before* you turned around to investigate the noise behind you. Is that correct?"

Matt nodded. "Yep."

Steve scribbled in his notebook. "And then,

when you looked back at the house, the bat was flying toward you?"

"Exactly."

"So, you never actually saw the bat come out of the bathroom window?"

Matt thought for a moment. "No. But where else could it have come from?"

"It could have come from anywhere."

Jenny held up her hand. "But what about Abby? She disappeared from the bathroom. If she's not turning into a bat, then how's she getting outside?"

"I wish I knew," Steve said. "In reality, we have no evidence that Abby is turning into a bat. Think about it. None of us have actually seen it with our own eyes. The only thing we do know is that she goes into the bathroom and a bat comes out."

"Yeah," Matt said. "A vampire bat. Named Abby."

Steve rolled his eyes.

Jenny shook her head. "Look, Steve, I know it sounds crazy. But what else could it be? If she's not turning into a vampire, then where's the bat coming from? And what happens to Abby?"

"I don't know," Steve admitted. "But I think, tomorrow, we should take a closer look inside the bathroom. Perhaps we can find a clue as to what's really going on."

Matt yawned and sprawled out on the bed.

"Sounds like a plan. Can we go to sleep now? I'm dead."

Steve agreed. It had been a long night for all of them.

Jenny stood and stretched. "See you guys in a few hours." She left, closing the bedroom door behind her.

As Steve lay in bed, he tried to come up with a possible solution. It could be that Abby was climbing out of the window as part of her sleepwalking. But how did the bat fit into all this? He scrunched his forehead in thought. Bats were nocturnal. It could be that a colony of them lived nearby, perhaps even somewhere in the house. That would explain their presence at night. And if Abby was opening the windows, it could be they were just flying in, taking advantage of the opportunity. Tomorrow, the Decoders needed to explore the entire house thoroughly, including the attic. The tricky part would be doing it without Abby or her parents questioning why.

The next morning, the kids gathered downstairs for breakfast. Abby's mom had made a giant stack of pancakes and sausage, and a large bowl of cut up fruit graced the center of the table. Once the kids began piling their plates, Mrs. Samson left them alone and disappeared up the stairs.

A woman came in carrying a bottle of juice. "Good morning, Abigail."

The girl smiled back and waved. "Hi, Janice. These are my friends, Steve, Matt, and Jenny."

"Good morning, children."

The trio returned the greeting. The housekeeper placed the juice on the table and retreated toward the kitchen.

"I'm glad you guys got to meet Janice. She usually doesn't come in on Tuesdays."

Jenny poured orange juice into her glass. "She seems nice."

Steve wiped his mouth with his napkin. "Why did she come in today?"

Abby shrugged. "I dunno. She's been coming in a lot more often lately. I don't know why."

As the group continued their meal, they tried to come up with a plan for the day.

"Since there isn't anything we can do about Abby's sleepwalking until tonight, I propose we focus on the missing jewelry items," Steve said.

Matt swallowed the large bite of food in his mouth. "What do you think we should do?'

Steve cut into the sausage link on his plate. "We should start by looking for clues around the house." Saying they were searching for the lost jewelry was a good excuse for them to snoop around.

"What kind of clues?" Jenny asked.

"Anything out of place. Abby, we're going to need you to help us with this." He needed to keep the girl distracted so they could search her room and bathroom without her getting suspicious.

Her face lit up. "You mean, I get to help you guys?"

Steve smiled. "Absolutely. In fact, we're counting on it."

"Yeah," Jenny chimed in. "You're really the only one who knows everything that's supposed to be here and where it all goes, so you'd be the first one to notice if something's missing or has been moved around."

Mrs. Samson walked in the room. "Abby, can I see you for a moment." Her face seemed upset.

"Sure, Mom." Abby got up and followed her mom up the stairs.

"I wonder what that's all about," Jenny said.

Matt looked up from his plate. "What what's all about?"

Steve pointed to the stairs. "Mrs. Samson. She appears to be upset about something."

Matt shrugged. "I didn't notice."

Jenny's eyes twinkled. "That's because there's food in front of you. I'm actually surprised you even noticed we're here."

"Ha ha. Very funny. But, you gotta admit, these pancakes rock."

Jenny nodded. "No doubt."

Steve was only partially listening to his friends. His mind was distracted by Mrs. Samson.

Something was definitely wrong. It could be about last night. She might have noticed they weren't in bed and saw them outside. He didn't know the rules of the house, but he was pretty sure that sneaking out in the middle of the night was not acceptable. Or, worse. What if she overheard their conversation about Abby being a vampire?

Within minutes, Abby came down. Her eyes were red and it was obvious she had been crying. She sat down at the table.

Jenny leaned over and hugged her. "Is everything okay?"

Abby shook her head. "Mom found one of the cufflinks Dad was looking for the other day."

"That's good, isn't it?" Matt said.

Abby's eyes swelled with tears. "It was in my nightstand drawer."

Jenny frowned. "How did it get there?"

She shrugged, wiping the tears off her cheeks. "I don't know. I swear. But, Mom doesn't believe me. When I told her I had no idea how it got there, she said something was wrong. The cufflink didn't get there on its own. Then when I started crying, she said maybe it was happening while I was sleepwalking. She's gonna call Dr. Hollister and ask if he has time to see me today." She looked scared. "Do you think it's true? Do you think I'm stealing stuff in my sleep?"

Steve thought back to the graphic novel in the

book store. *She couldn't help it. Jewelry was her only weakness.* He shook his head and frowned. "That doesn't seem likely. Why would you steal your dad's cufflinks? Or your mom's necklace? That doesn't make any sense."

Mrs. Samson walked in. "Dr. Hollister will be here in a half hour. Abby, you need to go get ready. Kids, would you mind waiting in the backyard? I'll have Abby come get you when he leaves."

The three detectives went outside and sat on the patio furniture on the deck. Matt clasped his hands behind his head and leaned back. "So, what now?"

Steve bit his lip. "Something's not right. It doesn't make any sense that Abby would be stealing her parents' jewelry."

Matt gave a short laugh. "Yeah, kinda like it doesn't make sense that she's turning into a vampire, too."

Steve stood. "Come on." He started walking away from the house.

Jenny jumped up. "Where are we going?"

Matt stood, a bit slower. "Please tell me it's not to spy on that doctor dude. I really don't wanna get arrested today."

Jenny smirked. "As opposed to any other day, when you don't mind if you get arrested?"

Steve held up his hand. "Focus."

"Okay, okay," Jenny said. "No more jokes. What's the plan?"

Steve stopped and looked up at the sky. "Now that we've got a little bit of time, I say we retrace our steps from last night. Matt, where did you first see the bat?"

Matt pointed. "Right up there, by the bathroom window."

Steve nodded. "All right. We'll have to check out the bathroom later. Then, once you started running—"

"In fear for your life," Jenny interjected.

Matt rolled his eyes. "Yeah, well, you'd be running, too, if there was a giant bat in your face."

Steve prompted, "Once you started running, which way did you go?"

He scratched his head. "Honestly, I wasn't really paying attention. I was just trying to get the bat away from me. But I do know that when the bat finally did leave me alone, I was close to the pool."

Steve nodded and started walking. "Let's head that way. Keep your eyes open for anything unusual."

The three kids followed the path to the pool. Steve studied the trees, the grass, and everything else along the way. Nothing seemed out of place or unusual. They reached the pool and spread out. Steve headed toward the lawn chair they had found Abby sleeping on. Something underneath it caught his attention. He reached down and picked up a shiny object.

"Guys," he called out. "Over here."

The other two kids walked over to join him. He showed them the small object in his hand.

"Is that…" Jenny started.

"…the other cufflink." Steve finished.

Matt picked it out of Steve's hand and looked it over. "Where'd you find it?"

"Under this lawn chair."

Matt looked down. "That's the one we found Abby in last night."

"Does this mean Abby really did steal the cufflinks?" Matt asked.

Steve shrugged. "I don't know. But I suggest we keep this to ourselves. Mrs. Samson already thinks Abby is a thief. I don't want to add any more fuel to the fire."

Jenny took the gold link out of Matt's hand and held it up to the sun. "What do we do now?"

"We keep searching. Somewhere out here there must be a clue to help us figure this out. Let's split up again and see if we can find anything."

The trio scattered. Steve headed back toward the house. Finding the cufflink was not a good sign. If Abby *was* stealing while sleepwalking, it could be very serious. The doctor might even suggest taking her to a special place for treatment. But something kept bothering him. Why would Abby steal these things? And what happened to Mrs. Samson's necklace and the other missing jewelry?

5 THE MYSTERIOUS FOOTPRINTS

Steve's investigation brought him to the back door of the house. He followed the outside wall, walking past the family room windows. The blinds were open and he could see inside. The downstairs floor appeared to be empty. He kept moving, focusing on the ground, searching for any evidence of an intruder.

Soon, he came across a set of footprints, but not by a door or window. He looked up and squinted in thought. If he wasn't mistaken, Abby's bathroom window was just above him.

He examined prints again. They were definitely adult, most likely male judging by the length. He put his own shoe up to them, hoping to be able to guess a size. Steve wore a size seven, and by the look of the indentations on the ground, he guessed the man who left them probably wore a nine or ten.

Reaching into his pants pocket, Steve pulled out his cell and took several pictures of the prints, along with his own shoe next to them. Satisfied he had enough documentation, he put his phone back in his pocket.

He continued his investigation but found no other footprints. Reaching the end of the back wall, he turned the corner and followed the side of the house, heading toward the front. Nothing. Not wanting to be seen, he turned around before reaching the front gate and searched the nearby trees and shrubs. Everything appeared normal.

When Steve arrived back at the pool, Matt was spread out on one of the lawn chairs and Jenny was sitting cross-legged, facing him, typing into her cell.

"Did you find anything?" he asked.

Jenny put her phone away and shook her head. "No."

"Me neither," Matt said. "How about you?"

Steve told them to follow him. He led them to the footprints he had discovered. "What do you guys think? Is that window up there the one from Abby's bathroom?"

Matt squinted up. "Yep. What do you think these footprints are all about?"

Steve shrugged. "I don't know. They're not yours, are they?"

Matt shook his head. "Nope. I never even got this close to the house."

"That's what I figured. What size shoe do you wear?"

Matt looked surprised and a little hurt. "Dude, I told you, they're not mine."

Steve suppressed a smile. "Put your foot next to one of the prints. I want to figure out the exact shoe size of the man that left them."

Matt's face relaxed and he put his shoe next to one of the indentations. "I wear a nine."

Steve studied the comparison. "Hm. I'm going to say our guest wears a ten."

"That's a pretty common shoe size, dude. Lots of guys wear a ten."

Steve nodded. "I know. But it's the only clue we've found so far, so we've got to make the best of it."

Jenny took a few steps back from the house and looked up. "There's no way anyone could climb up there from here. If these footprints belong to the thief, he didn't get in the house through that window."

"Maybe he was just out here casing the place," Matt suggested. "You know, kinda checking things out."

"That's possible," Steve agreed, then frowned. "But don't you think it's odd that we didn't find footprints anywhere else? Like near the backdoor or family room windows?"

"That's true." Jenny turned in a complete

circle, examining the grass around her. "If the thief was trying to find the best way in, there would be prints all over the place."

Steve bit his lip in thought. "What if the sprinklers washed them all away?"

The girl shook her head. "But then why would these still be here?" She pointed to the grass nearby. "There's a sprinkler about two feet away. It would've hit those footprints for sure when it turned on."

Steve nodded slowly. "Unless these prints are more recent. What if these were made last night?"

Jenny's eyes widened. "You think the thief was here last night?"

Matt shuffled his feet. Steve could tell something was bothering him.

"What is it, Matt?"

He shrugged. "I don't know. But, I mean, I don't wanna say…you know what, never mind."

Jenny crossed her arms. "Spit it out."

"Whatever it is," Steve added, "it could be helpful to the investigation. What are you thinking?"

Matt closed his eyes and took a deep breath. He exhaled slowly and opened his eyes. "I'm not saying I believe this, but what if Abby really is the thief, and she's working with someone else? Someone with a size ten shoe?"

Jenny looked up at the window and cringed. "I

guess she could easily drop stuff down here from her window. That would explain why the footprints are only here and nowhere else."

"That could also explain why Mrs. Samson found the cufflink in her nightstand," Matt continued. "She hides the stuff she steals in her room until her partner shows up at night."

Jenny bit her lip. "What do you think, Steve?"

He thought for a moment before answering. "I think your theory sounds possible, but we have other things to consider, too. For one, she's the one that asked Tyrone for help, remember? A thief wouldn't ask other people to come investigate when they're committing a crime."

"Good point," Jenny said, nodding.

"That's true." Matt sounded relieved. "And it doesn't explain the whole bat thing, either. And, even though you swear there's no such things as vampires, we saw one."

"We saw a bat," Steve corrected. "Another thing, none of Abby's actions indicate those of a criminal. Think about it. She got excited when we asked for her help. She was devastated when her mom accused her of being a thief."

"She was in tears," Jenny added.

Steve nodded. "Exactly."

Matt scratched his head. "So, if Abby's not the thief, which I'm totally glad she's not, then, who is? What exactly is going on here?"

Steve narrowed his eyes. "I think Abby is being framed."

"Framed?" Matt and Jenny repeated at the same time.

"By who?" Matt demanded.

Steve sighed. "I don't know, but it's the only solution that makes any sense. Abby didn't put the cufflink in her drawer, thus someone else did. Somebody *wanted* her mom to find it."

"But who would do that?" Jenny asked. "Who would want to frame Abby? And why?" She paused for a moment. "Could it be the maid, after all? I know Abby swears by her, but she could easily be taking stuff, then when the Samsons started noticing, she could've planted the cufflink in the nightstand."

Steve frowned. "But what about Mrs. Samson's missing necklace? It disappeared on a day the maid had off. And there isn't any evidence that the maid was here last night to plant the cufflink under the lawn chair."

Matt pointed at the ground. "I'm going with Mr. Ten Shoe Size."

Steve nodded. "I think that's a very good guess. Whoever this Mr. Ten is, he had to have been here last night. Nobody except us knows that Abby went to sleep out by the pool, so unless one of you two is trying to frame Abby, somebody watched us last night, knew where we had found her sleeping, and then put that cufflink there so it would be found today."

Jenny tossed her hands up. "Okay, that is super creepy. Are you saying we had a stalker last night?"

"Think about it. Mr. Ten might have been the noise Matt heard in the trees."

"Hey, yeah," Matt said, then scratched his head. "But if Mr. Ten is the guy that took the jewelry from the Samsons, then why was he here last night? Do you think he stole something else?"

"That'd be impossible," Jenny said. "The Samsons have already figured out that stuff's gone missing. I would think they have everything locked up good and tight by now."

"Maybe Mr. Ten didn't know they figured it out before he came out here last night," Matt suggested.

Steve held up his hand. "Hold on. I think we're looking at this all wrong."

"What do you mean?" Jenny asked.

"We're forgetting about the cufflinks. They were planted to make Abby look guilty. We should be focusing on why someone would want to frame Abby as a thief."

"Seriously, dude," Matt said. "She's eleven. Who would frame a kid?"

"I don't know," Steve admitted. "But if we truly want to help her, we must figure it out. The way I see it, there are a few things we need to do today. First, interview Abby. We should ask her to go back to when this whole sleepwalking problem started and go through her life, step by step, to see if we can discover any clues to help out with the investigation."

Matt shook his head. "I don't mean to be Mr. Negative or anything, but are you serious? I can't remember what I did two weeks ago let alone two months ago."

"Well," Jenny said, thrumming her fingers in her chin, "in your case, it really wouldn't be that hard. Eat. Sleep. Eat. Video game. Eat."

Steve laughed, then cleared his throat. "Next, I want to get up into the attic, and, if possible the roof, to see if we can locate any signs of bat activity."

"What exactly are signs of bat activity?" Matt asked.

"Residuals of food—"

"Hold on," Matt interrupted. "What are resi…residules?"

"Residuals are things left behind, left over, or remaining," Steve answered.

"Well, why not just say it that way, you know, in English?"

Steve rolled his eyes. "We'll look for any food *remains*, as well as signs of bat feces."

Jenny looked horrified. "Oh, no. No way. You are like totally on your own on that one. There is no way I am going anywhere to look for bat poop. That is sooo gross." She shivered.

Matt roared with laughter. Even Steve couldn't help but grin at Jenny's reaction.

Steve patted her on the shoulder. "It's okay, Jenn. Matt and I will take care of that part of the investigation. And while we're dealing with that," he paused and chuckled at the expression of disgust still on her face, "you can investigate Abby's bathroom. Look for anything suspicious. Somehow, that bathroom is the key to this whole thing."

"Got it," Jenny said, looking relieved.

Matt looked serious. "But be careful. We did find a bat in there, too. He might have left you a present." He burst out laughing again.

Jenny whopped him on the back of the head.

Steve pointed. "Here comes Abby."

The little girl walked up to them. Her eyes were swollen. "You guys can come inside the house now. Mom and Dad want to talk to you."

Jenny reached over and hugged the girl. "Are you okay?"

"No." She burst out crying. She sobbed in Jenny's arms for a moment then struggled to catch her breath. "I told Dr. Hollister everything—about how I think I'm turning into a vampire, and how I video-taped myself, and how I saw a bat coming out of the bathroom."

"What did he say?" Steve asked.

Her voice became shaky. "He said it was all in my mind, and that I was making this whole thing up. He looked really worried, too. I think he thinks I'm going crazy. Then, I told him that you all saw a bat; I told him the whole story you guys told me."

"What'd he say to that?" Jenny asked.

"He asked me to show him the video."

Steve nodded. "Good girl. What did he say when you showed him the proof?"

She shook her head. "I got my video camera, and…and…the video's gone. It isn't there anymore."

"What?" Matt said.

"That's impossible," Jenny said. "We all saw it."

Abby nodded. "I told him that. I said you guys would vouch for me, about the video." Her eyes filled with tears. "He said that, of course, you would, because you're really good friends. But it isn't real. It didn't happen." She paused and wiped a tear from her cheek. "Is that true? Are you guys just being nice to me? Am I losing my mind?"

Jenny hugged her friend again. "You're not losing your mind. We honestly did see the video."

"Yeah," Matt added. "We'll make sure to tell the doc, too. I mean, if you're crazy, then we're all crazy, and there's no way that I'm crazy."

"We-ll," Jenny said and chuckled. "That last part is kinda debatable."

"Hey," Matt said.

Abby half-smiled and wiped the remaining tears off her cheeks. "It gets worse. Dr. Hollister is moving in a couple days. Before he leaves, he's taking me to see some other doctor. They're gonna do a bunch of tests on me. He says I'm the one that's been stealing everything, but I've been doing it in my sleep and that's why I don't remember."

"We need to speak to the doctor," Steve said. "There's more to this story that he needs to know."

"He's in the house, waiting with my parents."

Steve nodded. "Let's go."

Jenny held Abby's hand in her own as they walked. "Don't worry. We've got your back."

They entered the house through the back sliding glass door. Abby's parents were sitting on the family room couch. A tall, slender man in a light gray suit sat opposite them on the loveseat.

Mr. Samson stood. "Kids, as I'm sure Abby has already explained to you by now, this matter has become much more serious than we originally anticipated."

Mrs. Samson cleared her throat. "I called my brother to come pick you up. He'll be here in about an hour."

"Pick us up?" Jenny asked, obviously surprised. "Why?"

"We're sending you home," Abby's dad said. "We have some things to work out."

"No!" Jenny said. "We want to stay and help."

Mrs. Samson smiled. "I'm sure you do, kids. But I'm afraid it is best for you to leave."

"Mr. and Mrs. Sampson," Steve interjected, trying to sound as grown-up as possible. "I do not believe you should make any decisions until you have all the facts."

"The facts?" Mr. Samson repeated. "What facts?"

"I believe someone is trying to frame Abby."

Mr. Samson frowned. "What?"

"Why would anyone want to frame an eleven-year-old girl?" The question came from the doctor.

Steve shook his head. "I don't know, but let's look at the facts. First, the video that Abby shot of herself disappeared off her camera." Steve lifted his hand before the adults could speak. "I know you don't believe it was there, but, I assure you, it was. We all saw it."

"Yeah," Matt said. "All three of us."

Steve continued. "Several items of jewelry have turned up missing, yet the only ones to resurface are the cufflink in Abby's nightstand, and this one." He pulled out the other cufflink from his pocket and placed it on the coffee table. "We discovered that outside this morning, under the lawn chair we found Abby sleeping in last night."

"Abby was out by the pool, again?" Mr. Samson asked.

Mrs. Samson shook her head, but said nothing.

"If Abby were stealing the jewelry, even subconsciously, it would only be logical that she would keep the stolen items in one place. Yet, nothing else has been found."

"Actually," Dr. Hollister said, tapping his chin with the pen in his hand, "placing items in various locations is common for kleptomaniacs, even those who do it unconsciously. Usually, a subconscious thief will hide the items in places that are important to them. For example, placing the cufflink outside may have some kind of significance to Abby. Perhaps she has a special memory of herself and her father near the pool."

Her dad nodded. "Abby and I spend a lot of time together at the pool. I could see how that's possible."

Steve frowned. "But why in her nightstand? What special memory would Abby have of her father in there?"

The doctor shrugged. "Only she could answer that."

All eyes turned to the girl. She looked scared. "I…I don't know."

Steve felt he was losing the crowd. "Back to the facts, we discovered something else interesting this morning while outside. There are adult footsteps, underneath Abby's window."

Mrs. Samson's eyes widened. "What?"

"Show us," Mr. Samson demanded.

Steve nodded and led the way towards the back door. It was natural for Abby's parents to be worried about a prowler outside their house, especially near their child's window. Perhaps, once they saw the footprints, they would take his theory more seriously. He pushed the sliding glass door open and stopped. The backyard sprinklers were on.

"No!" He ran through the spraying water to the place where they had encountered the footprints. He looked at the ground and winced. They were gone.

6 A NEW PLAN

The sprinklers turned off leaving Steve wet.

Jenny approached and looked down at the grass. "They're gone." Her voice sounded angry.

Steve nodded, drops of water dripping from his face.

Mr. Samson glanced at the doctor who gave a short nod. Steve knew exactly what that meant. No one believed them.

"Let's get inside," Mrs. Samson's voice said. "I'll get Steve a towel to dry off, then you kids should start getting your belongings together. Ty will be here soon."

As Steve followed the Samsons to the backdoor, he caught a glimpse of a man at the other end of the patio.

"Who's that?" He asked Abby in a low voice.

"That's Arturo, our gardener. He usually

doesn't get here until around noon. I guess he decided to come in early today."

The man stood motionless watching the group. Once they all entered the house, the sprinklers turned back on.

Steve bit his lip, deep in thought. The gardener that normally comes in the afternoon, showed up early and turned on the sprinklers, erasing any evidence of the footprints. The maid, who normally doesn't work on Tuesday, came in on a day she wasn't scheduled to, and has been working more often ever since the jewelry started turning up missing. Two possible suspects, definitely worth looking into.

While the Samson family waited downstairs with the doctor, the kids went up to their rooms. Steve took the towel Mrs. Samson had given him to dry off with and disappeared into the bathroom. He changed into dry clothes, threw everything he had into his suitcase, then met Jenny and Matt in the theater room with his bag.

Matt poured the last crumbs from a Doritos bag into his mouth, then wadded up the bag and tossed it in the wastebasket. "This whole thing stinks."

"Right?" Jenny said. "Nobody believes us."

"Can you blame them?" Steve sat on the sofa next to Jenny. "All our evidence is gone. Even the footprints. There isn't one shred of proof to back up anything we said."

"You know what the worst part is?" Matt said.

Jenny crossed her arms. "What?"

"They don't believe Abby. They're gonna send her to some kind of shrink, and she's not even crazy."

Jenny slammed a pillow down on the sofa. "And they're sending us away, too, so there's no way we can help her."

Steve scrunched his forehead. "*We* can't help her, but maybe the Decoders can."

Matt leaned back in the recliner. "What do you mean?"

Steve ignored the question. "How much money do you guys have on you?"

Matt looked surprised. "Huh?"

"I noticed a small motel not far from here," Steve explained. "I'm not sure if Tyrone will go along with this, but I'm hoping we can convince him to let us stay there. After all, our parents don't expect us back for a couple days. This way, we can sneak back here tonight without anyone knowing."

"I get it," Jenny said, her voice rising in excitement. "We can catch the thief in action. He won't be expecting us."

Steve nodded. "Exactly."

Matt grinned. "Get ready, Mr. Ten, 'cause you're goin' down!"

Steve held up his hand. "Don't get too excited. Tyrone may not go along with our idea, and we need an adult to check us in. So, back to my original question, how much money do you guys have on you?"

After counting their money, the trio decided that, according to the motel's website, they had just enough money between the three of them for one night.

"I'm glad it's a cheap motel," Matt said as they grabbed their luggage and began the walk down the hallway.

"Shh," Steve warned. "No more talk about that."

The doorbell rang as the kids joined the group downstairs. Tyrone came in and greeted everyone. After a few minutes of talking, Abby walked them outside. "Thanks for trying." Tears filled her eyes.

Jenny reached over and hugged her. "Don't give up. We know the truth."

They said good-bye and climbed into the car.

"Okay," Tyrone said as they pulled out of the driveway, "spill it."

Steve, with frequent interjections from Matt and Jenny, told him everything that had happened, from Jenny's first encounter with Abby's hissing to the doctor and the sprinkler incident.

Their friend shook his head. "I can't believe someone is trying to frame Abby. You can forget about trying to convince my sister and her husband, they need proof for everything."

"Speaking about that," Steve said hesitantly, "we have an idea, but we're going to need your help."

"Lay it on me."

He explained the plan, including how they would need his help to check into the motel. Tyrone pulled into a convenience store parking lot. He chose an isolated spot and put the car in park.

"Let me get this straight. You want me to leave you guys alone at some motel so you can sneak back when it's dark and catch a thief?"

Matt nodded. "Pretty much."

Tyrone said nothing for a few moments. Finally, he spoke. "There's another motel, a little bit past my sister's house. I think it might even be closer to her than the one you're thinking of, and I know the owner. I'd feel better if you all stayed there."

"Is it...affordable?" Steve wasn't sure how to ask how much it was going to be. They didn't exactly have an unlimited source of income.

"Don't worry about it," Tyrone said. "You're doing this to help my family. I consider this part of my fee."

Matt whistled. "Wow. Thanks, Tyrone."

"For sure," Jenny agreed. "That's like really nice of you."

The man held up his hand. "I do have one catch, though. Whatever you do, do not confront this Mr. Ten dude. You don't have any idea how dangerous he is. And I can tell you one thing for sure, if he's after my sister's jewelry, he could be extremely dangerous."

"Why is that?" Jenny asked.

He looked around and lowered his voice. "You know that sapphire turtle necklace that went missing?"

The kids nodded.

"That alone is worth about a hundred thousand dollars."

Matt gasped "A hundred thousand bucks? Holy guacamole!"

Tyrone nodded. "Tell me about it. I've been trying to convince them to get a security system for a few years now. They're just stubborn. Now, with that much money on the line, this thief could hurt anyone that gets in his way. So here's the deal. When you guys figure out who it is, get his description, take some pics, then get back to the motel and call the cops. I wish I could stay to help you out tonight, but I can't. I'm the MC for a big charity event. If I don't show, the event doesn't happen."

"That's okay," Steve said. "We'll be fine."

"Yeah." Jenny pointed to the three of them. "We're detectives, remember? It's what we do."

Matt put his hand on his heart as though trying to show sincerity. "And trust me, there's no way

I'm gonna go up to some crazy jewel thief and confront him. Last time we did that we ended up tied up in a hidden cave with a gun pointed at us. No…thank…you. I'm done with that." He was referring to the Decoders first case, The Magic Sapphire, in which an international jewel thief had tied them up after forcing them to find a hidden treasure for him.

Tyrone laughed. "All right, let's get you set up in that motel." He put the car in reverse and was just about to back up when Matt tossed his hands up.

"Hold on, hold on, hold on," Matt said frantically. "If we're gonna be camped out in a motel for the rest of the day, I'm gonna need some serious snackage. Think you can wait a few while I go inside and get some munchies?"

Tyrone agreed and the group went inside. After about twenty minutes, they walked out with bags of food and drinks. Before heading to the motel, Tyrone drove them to a fast food place for lunch where Matt swore over and over that the burgers were nowhere near as good as Tyrone's. Finally, at around one o'clock, their tall friend checked them into the motel. As they walked to their rooms, Tyrone glanced at this watch.

"I gotta jet. The diner's probably freaking out that I've been gone for so long." He handed the motel keys to Steve. "You all sure you're gonna be alright out here by yourselves?"

Steve nodded. "We'll be fine. And if anything comes up, we've got your cell on speed dial."

Tyrone nodded and waved good-bye. The kids walked into the boys' room. It was fairly small with two beds and a nightstand in-between. A long wooden dresser with a small TV on it faced the beds. Jenny rolled her suitcase through the adjoining door into her room and returned a couple minutes later.

She jumped onto one of the beds. "So, what's the plan now?"

Matt plopped on the other bed. "I vote for a nap. We only got about four hours sleep last night, and I'm guessing it's gonna be about the same, or even less, tonight. I'm dead."

Steve agreed. "I think we can all use some sleep. Besides, we've got hours before it gets dark." He yawned. "I say we sleep for a couple hours, then get up and come up with a plan of attack."

Jenny stood and stretched. "Sounds good to me. Goodnight." She walked through the adjoining door and closed it behind her.

Steve lay in bed, staring at the ceiling. They had to solve the mystery tonight. There was no way of knowing what time Mr. Ten would arrive, so it would be important for them to be there as soon as it got dark. Hopefully, they could get some good pictures of him with their cell phones. But even if the Decoders did figure out who the thief was and helped get back the stolen jewelry, it didn't solve the mystery they were hired to do—the case of Abby and the bat. He sighed, wishing there was some way they could check the attic. But the Samsons made it very clear they did not want the three kids there. He turned over in frustration. This would be the first case the Decoders didn't get to solve.

7 CAUGHT!

At four o'clock, Steve and the others got up and ate some snacks.

"So, what's the plan?" Matt said, as he stuffed a giant handful of potato chips into his mouth.

Steve swallowed a gummy worm. "We'll head over to Abby's as soon as it gets dark. I want to make sure we're there before Mr. Ten. And since we don't know *how* he's getting into the backyard, I suggest we each stakeout a different area." He crammed another few worms into his mouth.

Jenny took a sip of her bottled water. "Do you think I should text Abby and tell her what we're doing? What if she looks out her window tonight, sees us moving and thinks it's the prowler? She might run and tell her parents."

"Or call the cops," Matt added.

Steve nodded. "Good thinking. Do it."

Jenny whipped out her cell phone and her fingers flew over the keyboard. "Done." She reached over and took some potato chips out of the bag on the boys' nightstand.

Matt tossed his empty water bottle into the recycle basket. "So, let's say we see this Mr. Ten tonight. What are we gonna do? Follow him to see what he does, or take his pic and head back to the motel to call the cops like Tyrone said?"

"I say we stalk him," Jenny said. "We still don't know how he's getting in the house. If we can catch him in the act, we'll have more evidence to show the cops."

"I agree," Steve said. "We need to figure out as much as we can about what's going on before we call the police."

Jenny's phone beeped. She checked the text. "Abby says she's glad we're still on the case and wishes she could join us. She and her parents are going out to dinner tonight."

Steve perked up. "What time?"

Jenny typed into her cell. A few seconds later she received the response. "Around seven."

Steve's mind whirled together a plan. "Text back and ask if she'd be willing to leave the back sliding glass door unlocked. Let her know there's still some investigating inside the house we'd like to do."

"There is?" Matt asked as Jenny typed the text.

Steve nodded. "Yeah. We never got a chance to check the bathroom or the attic."

Matt chuckled. "Oh, yeah. The bat poop."

Jenny made a disgusted face, then her text alert sounded. "She'll slide the door open a smidge before they leave. We have to make sure it's closed all the way when we're done so she doesn't get in trouble." Jenny typed a quick response.

"Perfect." Steve grabbed the last gummy worm out of the bag. At least, they would get one more shot at solving the bat mystery.

Matt stretched out on the bed. "What's the plan for dinner?"

Steve shrugged. "It's not like we can really go anywhere."

Jenny jumped up and down on the bed, then sat down. "Won't it be great when we can drive? Think of all the cool mysteries we can solve once we're mobile."

Steve agreed. "We won't have to worry about people driving us around, or whether we'll have a ride to get anywhere."

"Yeah, that'll be great." Matt said, sounding borderline sarcastic "Now, back to my original question, which is the most important thing in the world right now, what's for dinner?"

Jenny lifted up a flyer lying next to the telephone on the nightstand. "How about pizza? They deliver."

Matt's mouth spread into a wide grin. "You just made my whole day."

After a brief argument over whether to get bell peppers on the pizza or not (which Jenny won with her 'extra veggies are good for you' statement), the kids called in the order and turned on the TV.

By six-thirty, the Decoders were ready for their mission. They all wore dark jeans and black hoodies, and each carried a small flashlight, in addition to their cells. Although their phones had a great flashlight app, they found it was more useful to carry a separate flashlight in case they needed to talk on the phone and search at the same time.

They left the motel and began the walk toward Abby's house. As they drew near, they heard a motor start and saw the garage door begin to rise.

"Hide," Steve whispered. Matt ran behind a giant tree, while Steve and Jenny crouched behind several trash cans.

Steve snuck a peek. The Samsons' minivan backed out of the driveway. In less than a minute, the vehicle drove past the kids. They waited a few to make sure the car didn't return, then walked into the backyard and slid the sliding glass door open.

Once inside, Steve closed the door. "I suggest we don't turn any of the lights on. It could alert the neighbors."

"Abby said she'd text when they were on their way home," Jenny said.

Steve nodded. "Good. We should plan to be done with our investigation in less than an hour anyways, so we can position ourselves outside to wait for Mr. Ten."

They turned their flashlights on and began climbing the stairs. Although it was still sunny outside, the inside of the house was fairly dark. The Samsons had all the blinds shut tight.

When they reached the second floor, Steve pointed toward their friend's bedroom. "Jenny, you check Abby's bathroom. Look for anything suspicious. Remember, she's getting out of there somehow. See if you can figure out how. Matt and I will go up into the attic and check things out there. Let's plan to meet in the theater room at seven-thirty."

"Got it." Jenny disappeared through the bedroom door.

Matt looked around. "Do you know where the attic is?"

Steve shook his head. "No, but the opening's got to be around here someplace." He shone the light on the ceiling and slowly walked down the hallway. Soon, he came to a section of the ceiling that could be removed.

"How do we open it?" Matt said.

Steve moved the flashlight beam around the section and located a ring. "I bet if we pull on that, it opens the panel. Can you reach it?"

The boy strained on his tip toes, but fell short. "Sorry, dude. I'm not quite there yet. But if I give you a boost, maybe you can grab it."

Once Steve agreed, Matt lifted him up. The small boy grabbed hold of the ring and pulled. Matt slowly lowered Steve, and the panel opened revealing a pull-down ladder.

Matt tugged and let the steps fall until they reached the floor. He shook the ladder to make sure it was stable. "Okay, let's do this."

Within seconds, the two friends were up the steps and in a giant room that appeared to run half the length of the house. Because the attic stood only four feet high, the boys had to duck.

Flashlights on, they swept through the area looking for clues.

"Dude," Matt said in a voice barely above a whisper, "check out all these boxes."

Boxes of all shapes and sizes were stacked around the room. Steve walked up to one. "This one's labeled, 'wedding stuff'."

Matt shined his light to a different stack. "Hey, this one says 'costumes'. Can we open it? I wanna see what kind of crazy get-ups they got. I bet they're all fancy."

"No," Steve said. "We need to focus on the mission. Look for bats or any evidence that bats have been here."

Matt grunted. "Party pooper." He grinned. "Get

85

it? Pooper? 'Cause we're looking for poop!" He laughed heartily as Steve rolled his eyes.

The two boys spent the next twenty minutes going over every inch of the large room, making sure to check every part of the roof and floor for possible clues. They found absolutely no evidence of bats.

"Dude, there's nothing here but a bunch of dusty boxes."

Steve scowled. "I know. We're no closer to solving the mystery than we were when we got here."

"Maybe Jenn found something."

Steve looked at his watch. "I hope so. Come on, it's almost seven-thirty now."

The boys backed down the ladder and lifted the panel back to its normal position in the ceiling. When they reached the theater room, Jenny was already sitting on the couch waiting for them.

"Did you find anything?" she asked.

Matt plopped down next to her. "Nope. Zilch. How about you?"

She nodded. "Oh, yeah. But I'm not sure you're gonna like it."

Steve sat on the other side of her. "What did you find?"

She held out her closed palm and opened it, shining her flashlight onto her hand.

Matt jumped up. "Whoa! Are those…"

"Teeth," Jenny finished. "Vampire fangs to be exact."

Matt's face twisted into a look of disgust. "That's so gross."

Jenny laughed. "They're not real, you moron. They're like the fake ones you buy at Halloween, only much nicer. These actually look real."

Steve took them out of Jenny's hand and held his light up to them. "Where did you find them?"

"In Abby's nightstand. I finished searching the bathroom pretty fast. There was nothing there. No secret way to get out. No vampire poop. Nothing. I even opened the window, but it'd be a pretty far jump to the ground. I really don't know how Abby's getting out of there."

She tied her hair into a bun. "After I finished the bathroom, I still had some time to kill, so I started looking around the bedroom. I figured I'd check the nightstand, since we know for a fact the thief had been there before. There's a bunch of junk in the drawer. The girl needs some serious organization skills. Maybe when this is all over I can come over here and help get her stuff together, or, at least, try to put some order to the chaos."

"Anyways," Matt prompted.

"Okay, sorry. So, I noticed this small plastic box. It looked out of place, like, way nicer than the other stuff in the drawer. I pulled it out and those were inside."

Steve handed them back to Jenny. "Abby must have put these on last night before she hissed at us." He frowned. "I don't understand."

Jenny shook her head. "Why would Abby want us to think she's a vampire? Was she trying to scare us?"

"Or, do you think what the doc said is true?" Matt asked. "Is she out of her mind?"

Steve bit his lip. "I don't know." He scrunched his forehead. "But one thing I am sure of, Abby doesn't remember doing this. I don't believe she was deliberately trying to scare us or hurt us."

"So, she *is* nuts?" Matt said. "Is that what you're saying?"

"I don't think she's crazy, either. These fangs are high quality, probably super expensive. Where would she get something like that? I think there's a big piece of this mystery we're missing, and until we figure that out, we're not going to solve it. Jenny, put the fangs back where you found them. Let's move to the backyard and get ready for our stakeout."

Once Jenny returned the fangs to their hiding place, the three kids walked down the stairs and out the sliding glass door, making sure to slide it shut tightly behind them. After that, the kids separated. Matt headed toward the far side of the pool so he could see if anyone came over the back wall. Jenny headed to the right of the house in case anyone tried to get to the backyard through that side, and Steve headed to the left for the same reason.

Once in position, Steve looked down at his watch. It was almost eight o'clock. He took out his cell phone and made sure his camera was ready to go. If Mr. Ten did indeed show up, the three kids decided they would first text each other his location, remain in hiding, then video tape him on their cell phones. Between the three of them, they should be able to get some incriminating evidence to show the police.

He studied the area around him. There were tall, wide trees that graced the gray block wall surrounding the property. Between the trees and the house were a series of large bushes. Steve decided to relocate behind one of those. As he settled in, he pulled up Google on his cell. He typed sleepwalking vampire into the search bar. A flood of sites came up, most of which had to do with vampires, some of which had to do with sleepwalking, but none that had to do with sleepwalking vampires.

Steve frowned. Why would Abby have put those fangs on? Even if she wasn't conscious of doing it, she still did it. Why? He asked Google what makes a person do something they don't know they're doing. One of the first sites mentioned hypnosis. That made Steve pause. Hypnosis. Abby mentioned Dr. Hollister using hypnosis on her to cure her sleepwalking problem.

He bit his lip in thought. Dr. Hollister was also leaving in a couple days and handing over Abby to another doctor to treat. He could be hypnotizing Abby to pretend she was a vampire. But why? Why try to convince an eleven-year-old girl she's a vampire?

He shook his head and scolded himself. Dr. Hollister was a respected child psychiatrist. The Samsons wouldn't have hired some quack. Steve's thoughts returned to the mysterious Mr. Ten. If he had to put money on it, he'd bet the gardener was behind it all. And possibly the maid. The prospect of the two of them working together was also a possibility. Hopefully, tonight, they'd find out the identity of the thief once and for all.

An hour passed and Steve received a group text from Matt: SOOO BORED

Steve smiled. Another text came in, this time from Jenny: ME TOO

Steve wrote back: THIS IS ONLY BEGINNING

He received two unhappy faces. As he started to type a return text, he heard a car in the driveway. The Samsons were probably returning from dinner. Within minutes, the lights in the house came on. A few moments later, Steve noticed the light in the upstairs hallway turn on. Abby was most likely now upstairs.

If the mysterious Mr. Ten was watching, he

would know that the owners were home. He texted his friends to keep their eyes open.

By ten-thirty, the downstairs lights turned off. Steve figured the Samsons had most likely gone to bed. He checked upstairs. The hallway light was off as well, but from his side of the house, he couldn't see Abby's room. He texted Matt, asking about the bedroom light. Matt said it had turned off about twenty minutes ago.

At eleven-thirty, Steve felt his phone vibrate. He read Matt's text: SOOOO BORED! KILL ME NOW!!

Steve replied: KEEP IT TOGETHER. OR THE BAT MAY KILL YOU.

DUDE, NOT COOL

Steve laughed.

Another half hour passed. Steve's phone buzzed again. He rolled his eyes and checked Matt's newest message.

ABBY JUST OPENED HER BEDROOM WINDOW

Steve perked up. He typed a quick text to both his friends: KEEP YOUR EYES OPEN. MR. TEN MAY ALREADY BE HERE.

Steve looked around, but saw no movement. He wondered if he should go join Matt. A couple minutes went by.

Another text came in: GET BACK HERE NOW!

Steve ran toward the backyard. As he turned the corner, he saw Jenny running from her side of the house. Matt was standing a bit further back, hiding behind a giant tree, waving them to join him.

Steve went up to him. "What happened?"

Matt pointed to the house. "I was keeping my eyes on the window while trying to keep my ears open for any sounds, you know, in case Mr. Ten was nearby. Then, I heard this flapping sound, and a bat flew over me and into Abby's bedroom."

"And?" Steve prompted.

"And, it's still there."

Steve looked up at the window. "That proves Abby is not turning into a bat. It flew *into* her room." He looked around the backyard. "I bet Mr. Ten is around here somewhere. Matt, keep your eyes on the window. Jenny, you go watch the left of the house, and I'll watch the right. Don't forget to check behind you, too. And get your cameras ready."

The kids obeyed and split up, determined to catch the thief once and for all.

Suddenly, Matt's voice boomed. "Look!"

Steve and Jenny whirled around just in time to see a bat flying out of Abby's window. The two kids filmed as the bat flew out of the window and in circles around the backyard. Matt kept his focus on the window.

Suddenly, the bat flew toward Jenny. She

shrieked and lifted her hands to protect her face. "Get away from me!" After a few moments, the winged creature finally left Jenny alone.

"I'm gonna follow it," Steve yelled.

He took off running toward the back, trying to keep up with the flying creature. He held his phone up, hoping to catch it on video. The bat made a few circles around the pool, then flew over the back wall and disappeared.

Out of breath, he returned to his friends.

"Are you okay?" he asked Jenny.

She nodded and shivered as though trying to shake away the memory. "Yeah, I'm good. What happened to it? Where did it go?"

Steve paused to catch his breath, then told his friends what he had seen.

Matt shook his head. "It's crazy that the bat went after Jenny. That's exactly what it did to me last night."

She shivered again. "That was super creepy."

"Hold on a second." Steve sniffed the air. "Are you wearing perfume?"

She thought for a moment. "No. But I do have lotion on."

"That reminds me," Matt said. "Do you have that lotion on you now? It smells so good."

Jenny reached into her back pocket and pulled out a small bottle. "Here you go."

As Matt poured a small amount on his hands,

Steve's eyebrows shot up. "Matt, did you have that lotion on last night?"

Matt returned the bottle to Jenny and rubbed his hands together. "Um, I don't remember."

"You probably did," Jenny said. "I had given you the bottle to hold, remember? You had it in your jacket pocket."

"Oh, yeah. That's right."

"Of course!" Steve said. "That's why it went after you guys. It's the lotion."

Matt looked confused. "Bats are attracted to lotion?"

"Not lotion," Steve answered. "Fruit. The one I saw tonight had large eyes, the characteristic of a fruit bat, not a vampire bat. And fruit bats are attracted to citrus smells. Your lotion smells like…"

"Mangoes!" Jenny said. "Okay, note to self: never wear lotion on a stake-out."

"There's something else," Steve fumbled with his cell phone. "Watch this."

He showed them the video he had taken. They watched the bat fly around Jenny's face, then fly away. He paused the video. "I'm gonna play it again. Tell me if you think it's got something in its mouth."

He played the video a second time.

"Yeah," Jenny said. "It does looks like there's something hanging from its mouth."

"Play it again, dude."

Steve nodded. "Let me see if I can make the image in the video bigger."

Jenny shook her head. "You can't. You can only pinch photos to make them bigger. It doesn't work with videos."

Steve scowled. "Too bad. We could really use a close-up of that."

"Hold on," Matt said. "Let's see if I've got one."

"You took pictures?" Steve asked, surprised.

"Yeah. I forgot to put it in video mode." He looked at the pictures on his camera. Most were terrible, but there was one that had a pretty good photo of the bat. Matt enlarged the image to be a close-up of its mouth."

Steve pointed. "There. It looks like something shiny."

Jenny took the phone out of Matt's hand and put the screen up to her face. "I think that's an earring."

Matt whistled. "More jewelry? Do you think Abby gave the bat that earring?"

Steve shrugged. "I don't know. Matt, are you sure it was Abby you saw open the window?"

He nodded. "Positive."

"And you're certain this bat, the one carrying the earring, flew out of her bedroom?"

"Yep."

Steve looked up at the house and bit his lip.

"Then, I don't see any other possibility. I'm just not sure she knows it's going on."

"You think she's doing all this in her sleep?" Jenny asked. "Like it's part of her sleepwalking problem?"

Steve looked at the back fence. "I don't know. Right now, I think we should try to figure out where that bat went. Come on." He started walking toward the side of the house. Matt and Jenny followed.

"Where are we going" Jenny asked.

"I want to go behind their house. The bat flew over the backyard fence. Let's see if we can figure out where it went."

They walked past the side of the house, into the front yard, and then around to the other side of the block wall. Because the Samsons lived on a corner lot, the kids didn't have to worry about trespassing on someone else's property. As they neared the end of the wall, Steve held them back.

He lowered his voice. "If it really was an earring we saw in the picture, then the bat probably flew over here to give it to someone."

"Mr. Ten," Matt said.

"Possibly. But we don't know that for sure. What we do know, is that Tyrone said Mrs. Samson's jewelry was worth a lot of money. So if there is someone back here, they could be dangerous."

Matt gulped. "Maybe we should turn back."

Jenny shook her head. "No way. This may be the only chance we have to see who's actually behind this."

"I agree," Steve said. "We just have to be careful."

The three kids snuck a look behind the Samsons' house. All they could see from the fence were trees. There were no houses. Apparently, the Samson house was right on the edge of a forest.

"Come on." Steve walked toward the trees.

They continued in silence. The only sound was the crunching of leaves from their footsteps.

Steve looked up into the trees. "Do you guys see any sign of the bat?"

"I don't see much of anything," Matt said. "Should we take out our flashlights?"

Steve thought for a moment. If Mr. Ten was anywhere around, he'd see the beams for sure and would probably take off. But on the other hand, as dark as it was outside, they couldn't see a clue if it stared them in the face.

"Yeah," he said finally. "Let's spread out and look for clues."

The three detectives took out their flashlights and began their investigation. Steve checked the nearby trees and ground for any sign of disturbance. After twenty minutes of searching, he came across tire tracks. He whipped out his cell and texted Matt and Jenny to join him.

Within minutes, all three kids were examining the tracks.

"What do you think?" Steve asked Matt who was quite knowledgeable with cars.

"They're pretty big. And deep. I'd say they were left by an SUV of some sort."

Steve nodded and pointed to the left. "You and Jenny follow them that way. I'm guessing they'll take you to the street. I'll go this way and see how close to the house they go."

After they split up, Steve kept his flashlight beam on the ground. They really had no evidence that this SUV had anything to do with their investigation, but it was the only lead they had. He followed the tracks for a few minutes then came to the place where the SUV had stopped and parked.

He looked up and saw that the backyard fence of the Samson house was within sight. He scrunched his forehead in thought. Whoever this thief was, they could easily drive here, release the bat to fly into Abby's bedroom, wait for it to return, and be gone in under fifteen minutes.

Steve frowned. But, why were there footprints next to the house? How did they fit into this? He shined his beam back to the ground and scanned the area. Something caught his eye. He walked over and reached down, pulling up a ballpoint pen. Steve stared at it for a moment, then his eyes widened. It all made sense!

He reached into his pocket to pull out his cell phone.

"Freeze." A deep voice cut into his thoughts.

Steve froze, his heart racing a million miles per second.

The voice spoke again. "Now, take your hand out of your pocket nice and slow, and put both hands up where I can see them."

Steve complied and turned around. There in front of him was Dr. Hollister, holding a gun.

8 MR. TEN

Steve's mind raced. If Matt and Jenny returned now, they would see the doctor and call the cops. The boy decided that if he could get the doctor talking it would make it easier for his friends to detect him.

He cleared his throat. "Why are you doing this?"

"Silence!" The doctor took the pen out of the boy's hand. He pulled Steve's hands down behind his back and slapped handcuffs around his wrists.

"I can't believe you framed Abby," Steve said.

"I said, silence!" The doctor pushed Steve down so hard it hurt his knees as they hit the ground.

He winced.

Dr. Hollister pulled a handkerchief out of his pocket and used it to gag him.

Steve's only hope was Matt and Jenny. Hopefully, they were out there right now, dialing 911. Soon, a voice sounded from beyond the trees. His heart sank. It was Matt. He was talking about a giant burrito.

Steve tried to yell for his friends to run, but the gag in his mouth kept him from making any kind of normal sound. He felt something cold touch his forehead and knew it was the end of a gun.

Helpless, he looked toward his friends. Jenny stopped in her tracks when she saw him. Matt was still talking, no clue as to what was going on. Finally, after babbling about a mound of guacamole, he noticed his friend.

Dr. Hollister spoke. "You two, put your hands high in the air where I can see them." They complied. "Now, come over here, nice and slow, or your friend gets a bullet to the brain."

The two kids walked slowly forward. The doctor threw a set of handcuffs on the floor in front of them. "Matt, cross your wrists behind you." The boy did as he was told. "Jenny, pick up the handcuffs and put them on your friend. Any wrong moves and your buddy here dies."

Jenny bent down to retrieve the handcuffs. She placed them on Matt's wrists and stepped back.

The man pointed to the ground with his gun. "Steve, lay down on your stomach. Matt, come here and lay face down next to him."

"Hold on," Matt said. "What about Jenny?" Matt was always protective of his best friend.

Dr. Hollister pulled another set of handcuffs from his back pocket. "Don't worry, she'll be joining you in a moment."

The two boys followed the instructions without taking their eyes off their captor. True to his word, he had Jenny put her hands behind her back and cuffed them as well.

"Now, boys, time to get up. The four of us are going for a little ride." He grabbed Jenny by the arm. "And just in case you get any ideas, I'll be holding on nice and tight to your girlfriend here."

The boys made no sound. They got up and followed the doctor through the trees. Soon, they came to a clearing and a parked dark blue SUV. Dr. Hollister opened the back passenger-side door. "Get in."

Steve walked up to get in first. The doctor reached into the boy's pocket, pulled out his cell phone, dropped it on the ground, and smashed it with his shoe. Steve attempted to climb into the tall vehicle, but without the use of his hands, he had trouble. Matt came up behind him and gave him a boost with his knee.

Before Matt climbed in, the doctor took his cell phone as well. The taller kid sighed. "I don't suppose I can convince you to ship that home to my mom?"

The doctor dropped the phone on the ground and smashed it with the heel of his shoe.

Matt cringed. "She's gonna kill me." He used momentum to get himself into the truck.

Dr. Hollister lifted Jenny inside, then slammed the door and locked it. The kids tried desperately to unlock the doors before the man got behind the wheel, but failed.

"Stupid child proof locks," Matt muttered.

The doctor climbed into the front seat and started the engine.

"Where are you taking us?" Jenny asked.

He said nothing.

"People will know we're missing," she said. "They'll be looking for us."

He still said nothing.

Mentally, Steve scolded himself. He had dismissed the idea of the doctor being the thief because of how much the Samsons trusted him. He shook his head. Never again would he make that mistake. From now on, everyone was a suspect, no matter how trustworthy they appeared to be.

He moved his head around trying to get the handkerchief out of his mouth. After a few minutes, he managed to move it out of his mouth. He licked his tongue against the roof of his mouth to moisten it.

Staring out the window, he tried to figure out where they might be going. With the dark tint of the

SUV's windows, it was difficult to see anything, but judging by the feeling in his ears, Steve decided they were going uphill. He felt a twinge of panic. If the crazy doctor took them up into the mountains, they might never be found. He looked over at his two friends. By the looks on their faces, they were thinking the exact same thing.

Dr. Hollister drove for another hour before the SUV came to a stop. The doctor got out and opened the door next to Steve. "Get out."

The small boy slid out of the vehicle and onto dirt. He looked around. They were at a cabin in the middle of the forest. Although it was too dark to see very far, he was pretty sure they were miles away from anyone.

Matt and Jenny slid out behind him.

Dr. Hollister closed the car door and motioned with his gun toward the cabin. "Let's go."

The three kids walked toward the front door. Steve strained his ears, hoping to hear even a remote sound of civilization, but only the crunch of their footsteps interrupted the silence of the forest. He walked up to the door and stopped.

The doctor came up from behind, put a key into the doorknob, and turned the handle. He motioned for the kids to enter. The trio walked slowly, trying not to run into anything. Soon, the door closed behind them and an overhead light came on.

Steve studied the inside of the cabin. The open

room where they stood was furnished sparsely, with only a small loveseat, an end table with a lamp, and a dinette set with four chairs. No pictures graced the walls, and there were no decorations of any kind anywhere to be seen. There was a small refrigerator, four feet tall, in the kitchen and a microwave on the small counter. A closed door on the far side of the room made Steve believe there was most likely a bedroom on the other side.

The doctor pointed to the dinette set. "Have a seat."

The three friends each took a seat on one of the chairs.

Jenny shifted around in her seat and grunted. "Um, do you think you could like untie us or something? This isn't exactly very comfortable."

The doctor said nothing, but grabbed Jenny's arms and uncuffed her left hand. He attached the open cuff to the rod connecting two legs of the table, then did the same to Matt and Steve. When finished, he sat on the fourth chair.

"I don't know how you kids figured out my plan, but one thing is for sure, I am not letting you ruin this for me. I'd rather not kill you, but I will if you get in my way. There's only one thing left for me to do. After that, I disappear forever. So, here's the deal. Once I'm safely out of the country, I'll anonymously call the police and give them the address of this cabin."

"When you're out of the country?" Jenny said. "When's that gonna be?"

"If all goes well, tomorrow afternoon."

"Tomorrow afternoon?" Matt repeated, horror in his voice. "We'll starve to death by then."

The doctor gave a short laugh. "Hardly. The human body can withstand much longer than a day or two without food. I should know, I *am* a doctor."

"But, we will need water," Steve said.

Dr. Hollister pointed to the sink in the kitchen. "The faucet works. If you work together, you can lift the table up and walk over to get a drink."

Jenny tried crossing her arms with her one free arm. "You can't just leave us here. People will know we're missing. They'll be looking for us." Her voice sounded angry.

"Yeah," Matt added. "And the last place they saw us at is Abby's' house, so that's where they'll start looking. Abby will tell the cops everything."

The doctor smiled, an almost evil look on his face. "Abby won't be in a place to tell anyone anything."

Steve frowned. "What do you mean?"

"I'm taking Abby to a mental facility today. That's the one thing I have left to do. I convinced her parents that she needed a serious psychiatric evaluation. So you see, it doesn't matter what she tells people, no one will believe her. Once I go with the Samsons to drop off their baby girl, I'll drive away, a bag full of jewels at my side, never to be seen again."

Steve felt his face get hot. "Why would you do this to her? Abby doesn't deserve this."

Matt struggled to get out of his cuffs. "Dude, when I get out of here, you are gonna be in a world of hurt."

The doctor smirked.

Steve really hated this guy. He took a deep breath to try and clear his head. Anger clouds thinking, he told himself. "Before you leave," he said, more in control, "could you at least answer a couple of questions?"

"Very well."

"First, how did you know we were out there tonight?"

The doctor crossed his legs and cupped his hands around his knee. "That's an easy one. I saw you walking along the side of the Samson house as I was driving away, and I knew you'd be snooping around for clues. I turned around and parked a distance away so you wouldn't see me."

Matt stopped yanking on the handcuffs. "But we didn't hear anything. I mean, we would've heard an engine out there. It was pretty quiet."

Dr. Hollister nodded. "The advantage of having a hybrid. When you go slowly, only the electric motor is needed. It makes no noise. Any other questions?"

"Yes," Steve said. "I suspect you are controlling Abby through hypnosis, but how are you doing it?"

"Now that's a better question. At each session, I put her under hypnosis. During one session, I would tell her what to steal. During the next, I would have her open the window for my trained bat to retrieve it."

Matt scratched his head. "But why have Abby wake up outside? Why not just have her go back to bed? Then, nobody would even suspect her of anything."

"Exactly," the jewel thief said and leaned forward. "You just answered your own question. I needed a reason to keep seeing Abby on a regular basis. Her sleepwalking was the perfect excuse to meet with her several times a week. Her parents insisted."

Steve scrunched his forehead. "Something still doesn't make sense. The vampire fangs. Abby woke up the other night, put vampire fangs on to scare us, then disappeared into the bathroom. Why? What good did that possibly do?"

The doctor laughed. "The fangs were just a bit of fun on my part. When Abby told me she was going to video tape herself, I decided to give her an even better reason to never get rid of me. You see, if she told her parents she was a vampire, they'd think she was crazy and keep me on, permanently.

But, she didn't tell them. Instead, she told you." His face darkened.

Steve started catching on. "You tried to scare us off by making us think she really was a vampire."

He nodded. "I programmed Abby to put on the fangs and lock herself in the bathroom. Then, I had her climb out the bathroom window and jump down to me. As I carried her to the lawn chair by the pool, I sent my bat into the bathroom to wait for you to open the door."

Steve nodded. That was why they found footprints under Abby's window. He was Mr. Ten. "And the second night?" he asked.

The doctor leaned back in his chair. "The second night, I had planned on a repeat of the first, but your friend," he paused and pointed to Matt, "standing outside complicated things. But then, when my bat came out of Abby's room, it went straight for his face." He chuckled. "You must have had some sweet smelling perfume on to get him that riled up. Once your friend disappeared trying to fight off the bat, I snuck out and had Abby jump down to me again. It worked out perfect."

Steve held up his free hand. "Wait. I still don't understand something. How did you get Abby to do these things? I get that you hypnotized her, but usually hypnosis has some kind of trigger. Abby was asleep. How did you do it?"

"I'm rather impressed you know so much about hypnosis," Dr. Hollister said. "During her sessions, I programmed her cell phone to go off at a certain time, then hypnotized Abby to do whatever I needed her to do that evening when she heard it ring."

Jenny slammed her hand on the table. "That's right! Remember? We heard that weird ringing just before Abby got up. I thought it was from far away, but her ringer was probably just on low."

"What about the cufflinks?" Matt asked. "How come you left them for Mrs. Samson to find? Didn't you think they'd get suspicious?"

The man frowned. "With a sleepwalking daughter? Why would they ever suspect me? In fact, I was the one who suggested it might be her."

"Which brings me back to this question," Steve said, his voice rising a little. "Why frame Abby? You are forcing her to go through a mental evaluation, when she's done nothing wrong. She thinks she's going crazy, her parents think there's something seriously wrong with her, and you're letting this happen. No, you're *making* this happen." The anger inside him was building.

The doctor laughed again. "I wouldn't worry too much about it. Once I'm gone, all her problems will be over. No more sleepwalking. No more bats. There's nothing wrong with her. The psych doctors will all confirm that. Even if she tells them her fears of becoming a vampire, they'll chalk it up to an overactive imagination. They'll send her home and, in a couple of weeks, everything will be back to normal at the Samson house." He smiled. "And I will be living like a king, somewhere far, far away where the laws of extradition can't touch me."

"The laws of what?" Matt said.

"You won't get away with this," Steve said, sounding much less confident than his words.

"Yes, yes, I will." He stood. "You see, there's nobody to stop me. You three are stranded here. There's thirty miles between this cabin and the closest house. And that's only *if* you're going in the right direction. If you head out into the woods in the wrong direction, well, they'll be finding your bodies in about four or five months. My suggestion, wait here. I will alert the authorities. Trust me. I'm your best hope of survival."

He pointed at his watch. "Guess I better be going. Abby's got a ten o'clock appointment with Dr. Rollings. I wouldn't want her to miss it."

The kids watched helplessly as he walked out the door.

9 STUCK IN THE WOODS

Steve watched Matt struggle with his handcuffs.

"What're we gonna do?" Matt asked. "We've got to get out of here and warn Abby."

Steve looked at his watch. "And we've only got about seven hours to do it. First things first. I don't suppose anybody happened to bring a paperclip with them?"

Jenny smiled and reached into her front pocket. She pulled out a large, silver paperclip. "Oh, yeah. After we got home from the movie set, I put a paperclip into the pocket of every single pair of jeans I own."

"Brilliant," Steve said.

"I know, right? Now, if I can just copy what Crazy Ben did, we're in good shape." She pushed her chair back and sat on the floor. After opening the paperclip, she stuck it inside the handcuffs' keyhole. On their last investigation, they had also been handcuffed and had been rescued by a nice man nicknamed Crazy Ben who freed them from their predicament with nothing more than a paperclip. Jenny was hoping to do the same thing right now.

Steve tugged on his restraints. "I don't suppose you have more than one paperclip, do you? That way we can all try to get out of these things."

Jenny shook her head. "Sorry. I didn't really think of that. But I'll make a mental note to put more paperclips in my jeans when I get home.

Steve and Matt waited while Jenny worked on the lock. She grunted. "Crazy Ben made this look so easy," she said, clearly frustrated.

"Just keep trying," Steve said. "Remember, we don't have any practice in this. And I know we said this last time, but I mean it when I say we need to invest in some handcuffs when we get home. All three of us should learn how to get out of these things quickly."

Matt gave a short laugh and leaned back in his chair. "No doubt, dude. I'm guessing this is gonna be a regular thing for us."

After fifteen minutes, Jenny finally managed to pick the lock. "Ha!" She jumped up and threw her handcuffs on the floor. "Take that, Dr. Hollister."

"Great work, Jenny!" Steve praised. "Now, it's our turn. Hand me the paperclip."

She shook her head as she walked up to him. "No way. I've got the hang of this now. It'll be faster if I do yours."

Steve nodded and let her work on his lock. It only took her seven minutes to undo his, and then another five to get Matt's.

As they stood rubbing their wrists, Matt pointed to the window. "It's still pitch black out. What time is it?"

Steve glanced at his watch. "Three-thirty."

Jenny walked to the front door and opened it. "Come on. We've got to get help."

Neither boy budged.

"What's the matter with you guys? We've got to get out of here."

Matt pointed outside. "Um, Jenn. In case you haven't noticed, it's dark."

She crossed her arms. "So? We've been out in the dark before."

"Not like this," Steve said. "We, literally, have no idea where we are. There's no telling how far we are from anything or anyone. And without our cell phones, we can't even call for help." He glanced at his watch again. "It'll start getting light in a couple of hours. I suggest we try to get some sleep, then leave at the break of dawn."

Jenny shut the door and slumped her shoulders. "I guess you're right."

Matt headed for the refrigerator, crossed his

fingers, and opened it. "Empty." He sounded disappointed.

Steve headed to the door he believed led to the bedroom. "Let's see if we can find some blankets."

The bedroom had one fold out futon and several blankets in the closet. The boys let Jenny take the futon and spread the blankets on the floor for themselves.

Matt snuggled under his blanket. "And to think, there's a nice, warm motel room bed with my name written on it laying empty tonight." Within minutes, he was snoring.

After setting the alarm on his wristwatch for six, Steve closed his eyes. How were they going to get out of this? If what the doctor said was true, they were miles away from anyone who could help them. They had no idea which way to walk, and they had no food. He sighed. And the worst part, if they didn't get back in time, Abby was going to end up in a mental ward.

The alarm went off at six o'clock exactly. It took Steve a few moments to remember where he was, but once he did, he jumped up. "All right, guys. Get up!"

Matt groaned and pulled the blanket up over his head. "Just a few more minutes."

Steve pulled the covers off his friend. "Get up. We have to save Abby."

That got Matt and Jenny up in a flash. After

taking turns freshening up in the restroom, they took a deep drink of water, then headed outside.

The sun had not yet risen, but the hint of daylight was enough for them to see their surroundings. Tall pine trees stood in every direction. They were definitely in the middle of the forest.

Jenny spun in a complete circle. "What should we do?"

Steve pointed to the ground. "I say we follow the tire tracks. At the very least, they'll take us back to a road. Perhaps, if we're lucky, a car will drive by and spot us. At any rate, I think we have a better shot of being found that way than if we took our chances in the forest."

The others agreed and they began their trek through the wilderness.

Matt patted his stomach. "Man, am I hungry.'"

Jenny whimpered. "Please don't talk about food. I may cry."

"You?" Matt gave a short laugh. "How about me? I usually eat something every hour. I live for food. It's my life."

Steve decided to intervene before they got into some long, drawn-out argument over who needed food more. "How about instead of talking about food, we focus on what we're going to do once we're rescued."

Jenny slid on some loose pebbles. "Whoa.

Watch those rocks. I think the first thing we should do is call the cops. They can go straight to the Samson house and arrest Dr. Hollister when he shows up to pick up Abby."

"What if it's too late?" Matt said. "What if we're not rescued until after ten?"

"Then, we tell the cops to call the Samsons, find out where they are, and meet them there," Jenny answered.

Steve frowned. "You're both assuming that the police are going to believe us."

"Why wouldn't they?" Matt asked.

"Because we're twelve," Steve said. "Unfortunately, kids crank call the police all the time."

Jenny bent down to tie her shoe. "So, how are we gonna call the cops, anyway? We don't have our cells."

Matt stopped to wait for his friend to finish with her shoe laces. "Maybe whoever rescues us will let us use theirs."

Steve leaned against a nearby tree. "That would be ideal. And if they do, we should plan to call Tyrone."

Jenny stood and clapped her hands. "That's a great idea! We can tell him everything and he can call the cops. They'll believe him for sure."

"That is, of course, if we are rescued," Matt said, gloom in his voice. "Anyone else notice that there aren't any other tire tracks on this road except the doc's?"

Steve resumed walking "I noticed. But we did get to the cabin from a main road. Once we get there, hopefully, we'll run into someone."

Matt grunted as he followed his friend. "Do you remember how many cars we passed last night as we were driving here? I do. The answer is zero."

Steve tried to sound optimistic. "That's true, but it was one in the morning. I wouldn't expect there to be any cars out here that late. Now is the time when people start going out for hikes and nature activities."

Matt's eyes widened. "Dude, you're right. This is about the time my dad and I would start heading out."

"See?" Steve said. "So, all we have to do is get to the main road."

They continued the walk in silence. After a while, Steve glanced at his watch. It was already seven-thirty. Time was running out.

Matt suddenly stopped. He motioned for the others to do the same.

"What's wrong?" Jenny whispered.

"Shh," he whispered back. "Listen."

Steve strained his ears. Then, he heard it. Snapping twigs.

Jenny took a step closer to Matt and pointed to the forest on their right. "Somebody's out there."

Matt nodded. "Yep. What if it's the doc, coming back to finish us off?"

Steve shook his head. "He wouldn't be walking in the forest. He'd be in his SUV on this road."

The kids stood frozen, waiting to see what happened. Soon, a college age boy appeared through the trees. He wore hiking pants with tons of pockets, an olive green T-shirt with a hoodie wrapped around his waist, and a sturdy, large backpack. He waved at the kids and walked toward them.

"Ahoy!" he yelled out.

"Hey," Matt greeted.

The young man grinned as he approached the trio. "I didn't expect to see anyone out here so early." He frowned as he appeared to study them. "Where's your gear? Or water? Why aren't you carrying any water? That's not very smart."

Matt sighed. "Trust me, dude, not our idea."

"Do you have a cell phone we can borrow?" Steve asked.

The man shook his head. "Sorry. There's no service way out here, so I don't carry it with me. Is there something wrong?"

Steve decided it best not to give away too much information. "Let's just say, we're pretty much lost. Do you have any idea how far it is to the main road? We need to get to a telephone."

The hiker pointed to the path they were taking.

"If you keep going up that way, it'll be about ten miles or so till you get to the road. You probably won't have to wait too long before a car drives by. Especially with this amazing weather. Everybody and their grandmother will be coming out here today. But if what you're looking for is a phone," he paused and pointed to the forest behind him, "there's a ranger station about two miles west of here. Nobody's stationed there, but it's always open for hikers, and they have a phone. If you keep heading west, you'll run right into it."

"West?" Jenny sounded nervous. "What if we make a wrong turn? We could be wandering around the forest all day."

The young man laughed. "I wouldn't worry about that." He pointed to the sun, which was rising in the sky behind them. "As long as you keep the sun behind you, you'll be okay."

Steve nodded. "Because the sun rises in the east."

The hiker grinned. "Exactly. Besides, in about a half-mile or so, you'll see a worn-out foot path. Just follow it west, and it'll take you straight to the ranger station."

The kids thanked the man and began their journey through the forest.

Matt swatted a fly away from his face. "I sure hope he knows what he's talking about."

Jenny ducked to avoid a low-hanging branch.

"He looked like he really knew the area. And honestly, I was getting tired of that road. It felt like it was gonna go on forever."

Steve agreed. "In addition to the phone, the ranger station will also most likely have a water fountain we can use."

Matt crossed his fingers. "Any chance it'll have food?"

Steve laughed. "Don't count on it."

They walked the next half-hour in silence. Finally, Matt pointed in front of him. "Hey, I think I see the path."

Keeping the sun behind them, the kids followed the trail west.

Matt jumped over a large rock. "I don't know about you guys, but I feel a whole lot better now that we're on an actual trail."

The others agreed and continued their walk in higher spirits.

In another forty-five minutes, they saw a structure through the trees.

Jenny squealed in excitement. "We found it!"

The kids rushed up to the building which was the size of a small cabin. They walked through the door and looked around. A large map of the area covered one wall and a display of various types of birds covered another. Toward the back was a long table with pamphlets. Behind the table was a chair, and next to it, on a small table, sat the telephone.

Matt picked up the receiver. "Please work." He held it to his ear and grinned. "Houston, we've got a connection."

Steve heaved a sigh of relief. "Call Tyrone." He glanced at his watch. "It's almost nine o'clock."

Matt went to dial the number and froze. "I…I don't have his number memorized."

Jenny gasped. "Me neither. I didn't even think of that."

"It's okay," Steve said. "I know it."

He told the number to Matt, who then pushed the speaker phone button so they could all participate in the conversation.

The phone rang three times, then went to voicemail. "You've reached Tyrone. If you're hearing this, it's cause I've got other stuff going on. Leave a message, and I'll get back to you."

Steve snatched the phone and held it up to his mouth. "Tyrone, it's Steve. Our cells are gone and we need to talk to you ASAP. Abby's in trouble. Call your sister and tell her not to let the doctor take Abby. He's the thief, and he's very dangerous. We're at a ranger station in the middle of the forest. The number here is…," Steve looked at the phone, "…five-five-five-seven-three-eight-two-four-four-five. Call us back after you've called your sister." He hung up.

"What do we do now?" Jenny asked.

Steve stared at the phone. "We wait."

10 WHAT TO DO?

Steve continued to stare at the telephone. He could feel his heart racing in his chest.

Matt ran his hand through his brown hair. "What if Tyrone doesn't get our message in time? What if it's too late?"

Steve took in a deep breath and exhaled slowly. That same thought ran through his head. But they needed to stay calm. "There's nothing we can do right now. When Tyrone calls back, he's going to ask us where we are. And since we don't have our cells, we need to figure it out the old fashioned way." He pointed to the giant map on the wall.

The three friends crowded around the map. Matt put his finger near the center. "Here's the 'you are here' picture."

Steve nodded. "Okay. Now, let's figure out where the nearest road is to our present location."

Jenny pointed. "Up here. Route 999. How far do you think that is from this cabin?"

Steve studied the map until he found the legend. "According to this, an inch is equivalent to a half-mile."

Jenny used her thumb from the tip of her fingernail to the knuckle to measure. "I'd say it's about three miles to the road."

"Then, how far to town?" Matt asked.

She shrugged. "It doesn't really show any towns on here."

Steve scrunched his forehead. "We were in Dr. Hollister's SUV for a total of an hour-and-a-half from Abby's house to the cabin. We may be a bit closer now, so it's a good guess to say we're like an hour to an hour-and-fifteen minutes from town."

The phone rang and all three kids jumped in surprise. Steve ran over and picked up the receiver. "Hello?"

"Where are you guys?" Tyrone's voice boomed.

Steve put it on speaker phone.

"Tyrone," Steve said, "did you get a hold of your sister?"

"No. I left three messages on her cell. Her husband's not answering his phone either. I left messages on his cell, Abby's cell, their landline, I even called my mom and told her to try getting a hold of Denise."

Jenney stomped her foot. "We're too late!"

"You need to tell me exactly what's going on," Tyrone said.

Steve, with loud and frequent interruptions from Matt and Jenny, related everything that had happened since he left them at the motel.

"What was the name of that psychiatrist Dr. Hollister is taking Abby to? Maybe I can track him down."

"Dr. Rollings," Steve answered. "And her appointment is at ten o'clock."

"Got it. Listen, I need to get off the phone and try to find Abby. I'll come get you once I track her down. You're all okay up there, right? No bears or mountain lions?"

"Or food," Matt grumbled.

Tyrone laughed. "I promise I'll bring you something to eat when I come up."

Steve cleared his throat. "Will you call us when you find anything out?"

"I promise."

The kids said good-bye and wished him luck.

Matt sat down, resting his head against the wall. "So, what are we supposed to do in the meantime?"

Jenny plopped down next to him. "I don't know, but I feel so useless. I hate not having a cell. It's like, I have no idea what to do."

Steve chose to sit facing his two friends. "You

know, this is how life used to be. Our parents didn't have cells growing up."

Jenny rolled her eyes. "Whatever. My dad reminds me of that all the time. But come on. This is the twenty-first century. I like live on my phone. For reals."

Steve muffled a laugh, because he knew it was true. Jenny's whole existence centered around her phone.

"Speak for yourself," Matt said. "I really only use mine to text you guys. And my mom." He winced. "Oh, man. She's gonna kill me for losing another one. And I can't even tell her it wasn't my fault this time."

Jenny's blue eyes twinkled. "Sure you can. You can be like, 'hey, Mom, look, this psycho jewel thief took my phone and smashed it into the ground before he kidnapped me at gunpoint and took me to a cabin in the middle of the forest'."

"Where he left me to die," Matt added. "Without food."

The three kids laughed.

Jenny leaned forward and hugged her knees. "Can you imagine what our parents would say if they knew what we've really been doing this summer?"

Matt gave a short laugh. "Are you kidding? My mom would lock me in my room and throw away the key."

Jenny giggled. "I know, right? My dad would ground me until I was like thirty."

"How about you, Steve?" Matt asked. "What would your parents do?"

He said nothing.

"Steve?" Matt repeated.

"Why aren't the Samsons answering their phones?"

Jenny shrugged. "They're probably on their way to see that Dr. Rollings guy. I know my dad doesn't answer his phone either if he's driving."

Steve frowned. "But wouldn't he answer it if he noticed his sibling calling him multiple times? I mean, if anyone called me three times in a row, I would know it must be something important."

"That's true," Jenny said. "I remember one time, I lost my purse at the mall, and I called my dad twice back to back and left messages. He called me like right back."

Steve nodded. "Exactly. Tyrone left messages for them to call him back immediately. What would keep the Samsons from returning his call?"

"Maybe they have their ringers off," Matt suggested. "I know whenever my mom takes me to the doctor or dentist or whatever, she makes me silence my phone. I bet that's what they did. They probably haven't even noticed that Tyrone called."

Steve pointed to his watch. "It's only nine-twenty. Abby's appointment isn't until ten."

"They probably went there early," Jenny said.

Steve said nothing. Something was wrong. He could feel it. He picked up the phone and dialed Tyrone's number.

"Hey," Tyrone answered.

Steve put it on speaker phone. "Tyrone, I think something's wrong."

"Tell me about it. I couldn't find anything on this Dr. Rollings guy, so I called my friend over at UCLA. Guess what I found out? Dr. Rollings got kicked out of his practice about a year ago after several clients claimed he had been stealing from them. Nothing was ever proven, but the psych center he worked for decided to let him go. And get this. Dr. Rollings' partner at the psych center was none other than Dr. Robert Hollister."

"So, if Dr. Rollings doesn't work at the psych center anymore, then where is Dr. Hollister taking Abby?" Steve asked, his heart sinking.

"I don't know, but I just got off the phone with the cops."

"And?" Steve prompted.

"And, nothing. I talked to my buddy Roland down at the precinct. Unfortunately, since Abby and her parents haven't been missing for twenty-four hours, I can't file a missing persons report."

Steve shook his head. "But Abby's been abducted. Can't they put out an AMBER Alert or something?"

Tyrone sighed over the phone. "Only if one of her parents calls the precinct and reports it."

"But what if her parents have been abducted, too?" Jenny said.

"There's nothing the police can do. At least, not for twenty-four hours. Listen, I'm about to get out of here and come get you guys. Tell me exactly where you are."

Steve related their location, stating that they would leave immediately and hike the three miles out to Route 999.

Tyrone typed it into his phone and estimated that he would be there in approximately an hour and ten minutes.

The kids hung up and departed to begin their hike through the forest.

Jenny pulled her hair into a ponytail. "Where do you think they are?"

Steve shrugged. "I wish I knew." He scrunched his forehead. "Let's try to reconstruct everything that happened last night, from the minute he kidnapped us to the moment he left. Perhaps something he said can give us a clue."

Jenny nodded. "Okay. Let's see. Steve, you were the first one he made contact with. What did he say to you before we got there?"

The small boy thought back. "He told me to freeze and put my hands up nice and slow. Then, I tried to get him to talk so you guys would hear us and call the cops. But he refused, and put a gag in my mouth."

Matt moved a branch out of his way. "Then, Jenny and I walked up—"

"And Matt was going on and on about some burrito," Jenny interrupted.

Matt grinned. "It was a pretty great burrito. Okay, so we walked up and he told us to put our hands up or he'd put a bullet in you."

The three friends took turns recanting the long ride to the cabin and the doctor's insistence that they not speak. Once they were inside the cabin, the kids agreed he seemed more at ease. He even volunteered to answer questions.

"Let's think about the questions," Steve said.

"We asked why he was framing Abby, and he said she wasn't actually in any real trouble," Matt recalled.

"That's right," Jenny said. "He said the psych doctors would clear her, and in a couple of weeks, everything would be back to normal at the Samson house."

Matt scratched his head. "Do you think he was lying to us? I mean, if that Dr. Rollings dude isn't for real, then the two of them could be kidnapping Abby and her parents together."

"Maybe they're planning on holding the three of them for ransom," Jenny said.

Steve frowned and bit his lip. Something about

that theory was off. "I don't know. Dr. Hollister seemed sincere when he said the Samson household would be back to normal. I think he was telling the truth."

"But then, what happened to them?" Jenny said.

Steve scrunched his forehead. "Something must have happened between the time he left us and the time he went to pick up Abby."

"Something like what?" Matt asked.

"That's what we've got to figure out. And fast."

11 HOSTAGES

They continued their walk in silence. Steve thought furiously. What could've happened? Perhaps, Dr. Rollings came up with a new plan that did indeed involve holding the Samsons hostage. But why kidnap all three of them? They'd really only need Abby. Her parents would undoubtedly pay a great deal of money to get her back. And it would be a whole lot easier to kidnap an eleven-year-old girl than a whole family.

"You know, there's another possibility," Jenny said, interrupting Steve's train of thought

"What's that?" Matt said.

She stopped a moment to pull up her socks, then jogged to catch up to the boys. "What if the facility they took Abby to doesn't have good reception? Then, they wouldn't even know that Tyrone had been calling."

"That's true," Matt said. "And you know what else I've been thinking?"

"You've been thinking?" Jenny joked.

Matt threw her an evil look. "I'm being serious here."

"Sorry, go on."

"Remember last year when my grandma was real sick and we went to the hospital? They made us all turn our cell phones off. What if the doc really did take Abby to a medic place and they made them all turn off their phones? Then they wouldn't know if anyone's been calling."

Steve nodded. "Both of those are good possibilities. The big question is, if Dr. Hollister knows that Dr. Rollings is no longer employed, then where is he taking her?"

Jenny held up her hand. "Hold on. We don't actually know that Dr. Rollings isn't employed. We just know he got booted from that one place. Who's to say he hasn't found a job somewhere else? Ugh. If we had our cell phones, we could Google him."

Steve shook his head. "Tyrone would've already done that. And if he couldn't find him, I don't know how we're going to."

After forty-five minutes of walking, the trio made it to Route 999.

Steve looked down the road and squinted. "Now, all we have to do is wait for Tyrone."

Matt swatted away a fly. "And then what?"

Steve thought for a moment. "I think our best course of action is to have him take us back to Abby's house. It might be that they left a clue behind as to where they went."

Jenny crossed her arms and stomped her foot. "I hate not having a cell phone. We could totally be calling all the mental facilities in the area seeing if Abby is there."

Steve chose a large rock and sat on it. "I don't think the mental facilities would give us that information. Patient confidentiality." He paused and scratched his chin. "On the other hand, they would be able to tell us if they had a Dr. Rollings that worked there."

"See?" Jenny said. "We could so be doing that right now. I seriously don't know how people lived before cell phones were invented. I would literally just die."

Matt groaned. "You mean like I'm going to when I tell my mom I lost another one? She's seriously gonna kill me. Or worse."

Steve sympathized. He knew how Matt felt. He was also wondering how he was going to break the news to his parents. "We need to come up with a story about what happened to our cells, in case our parents ever talk about it to each other."

Matt laughed. "You mean we're not going to say that a crazy jewel thief kidnapper stepped on our phones so we couldn't call for help?"

"I'm serious." Steve stood. The rock was not very comfortable. "What should we tell them?"

"We could say we lost them at the movie theater," Jenny suggested.

Matt shook his head. "Nope. I already did that."

The girl stared at him. "You lost your phone at a movie theater?"

"Yeah. I had it in my pocket and it slipped out when I sat down. I didn't notice till I was outside getting ready to call my mom. By the time I went back to look for it, it was gone."

"Bummer." She sounded sincere.

"Tell me about it."

"Okay, so no theater," Jenny said. "Then, how about the community center? We could say we put our stuff down and when we went back to get it, our phones were gone."

Matt held up his hand. "Done that."

Jenny tossed up her hands. "Are you kidding me?"

"Nope. I was playing basketball, and when I went back to get my stuff, my phone was gone."

"Exactly how many phones have you lost?" Steve asked.

"Including this one? Five."

"Five!" Jenny looked horrified. "No wonder your mom's going to kill you."

"I know. I'll be lucky if she even gets me a new one. She'll probably—"

"Hold on," Steve interrupted. "A car's coming."

A large blue, four-door sedan came into view. The vehicle slowed down as it neared the kids, then stopped in front of them.

"Hop in," Tyrone's voice came from the driver's side.

Steve climbed into the front while Matt and Jenny slid into the back.

"Thanks for coming to get us," Steve said as their friend made a U-turn.

"Are you kidding? I'm the one that got you all into this, remember? Which reminds me…Matt! Open up that duffle bag on the floor by your feet.

Matt did as he was told and looked inside. "I've never been so happy in my whole entire life." Inside the bag were sandwiches, chips, cookies, and a variety of other snacks.

Tyrone laughed. "And Jenny, that cooler down by your feet has some sodas and bottled water."

The kids thanked their friend over and over as they distributed the food and drinks. Steve told him about the plan to go to Abby's house and search for clues. He agreed.

The remainder of the journey was fairly quiet. The kids ate and, occasionally, Tyrone would chat about something happening in town.

As they pulled up to the house, Steve pointed to the carport. "The minivan's missing."

"So, wherever they are, they're in Mrs. Samson's car," Matt said as he got out of the blue sedan.

"How are we gonna get inside?" Jenny asked.

Tyrone pulled something out of his shirt pocket. "I got this. Denise gave me a key when they moved in. Come on." He led the way up the path to the front door.

Once inside, Steve studied the interior of the house. Nothing looked disturbed and there were no signs of a struggle. If the Samsons were kidnapped, they went willingly. "Let's spread out. Jenny, you and Matt check upstairs. See if you can find something in Abby's room. Tyrone and I will look around down here."

"Got it!" Jenny said and the two of them headed up the stairs.

"What should I be looking for?" Tyrone asked.

"Anything that could give us a hint as to what happened this morning. Perhaps an address or phone number, or something that looks out of place."

Tyrone nodded and left to go check the family room. Steve studied the front living room and noticed a glass of water on the coffee table. It was still cold and a couple of lingering ice cubes floated on top. Somebody had put this glass on this table not that long ago. The Samsons definitely had a guest, and if it was Dr. Hollister, then chances were high that they were with him now. Something in this house had to hold the clue to where they had gone.

"Yo, Steve," Tyrone called out. "In here."

Steve rushed to the family room. "What is it?"

Tyrone pointed to the computer. "It's still on. No way would my sister or her husband leave the computer on like this."

"Can you tell what they were looking at?"

Tyrone shook his head. "Nope. No programs are open. They could've been doing anything."

Steve had an idea. "Can I borrow your cell phone?"

After Tyrone handed it to him, Steve immediately dialed a number.

"Hello?" A female voice answered.

"Hey, Alysha. It's Steve. I need a favor."

Alysha Stonestreet was the Decoders best secret weapon. A computer whiz who could find her way around the internet better than anyone alive, she had been an invaluable help to the Decoders on both their previous cases, and Steve hoped she could help them one more time.

"Steve?" she said. "Where are you calling from?"

"This is Tyrone's phone. Listen, I don't have time to explain everything right now, but the Decoders need your help immediately. Lives may depend on it."

"Okay." She sounded nervous. "What do you need?"

He quickly explained their concern for Abby and her parents' safety.

"The computer's still on and we think perhaps there's a clue on it somewhere. Do you think you can help us?"

"I can try." Alysha then had Steve log onto the internet and talked him through finding the browsing history to see what had last been researched.

Soon, Steve came to an interesting website. "Hold on," he said as he opened the site. "It's an article about Dr. Rollings." He read through it quickly. "It talks about him losing his position at the clinic a year ago." He looked up at Tyrone. "If your sister saw this, she may have questioned Dr. Hollister about it when he got here this morning."

Just then, Matt and Jenny walked in and Matt placed a few objects on the desk next to the computer. "We know why they aren't answering their cell phones." He pointed. "They're all right here."

Steve glanced at the three phones. "Where did you find these?"

"They were on Abby's bed," Jenny said.

Steve frowned. "That's a weird place to find them."

"Maybe not." Tyrone turned the computer

monitor to face the kids. "Check out what else my sister was looking up."

The three kids stared at the screen. There was a twenty-year-old newspaper article with a picture of a young Dr. Hollister and the headline DOCTOR ACCUSED OF JEWEL HEIST ACQUITTED FOR LACK OF EVIDENCE.

Steve shook his head. "The Samsons must have figured out that he was the one stealing their jewelry. I noticed a glass of ice water in the living room. Here's how I'm thinking it played out. Dr. Hollister arrived this morning. Mrs. Samson let him in and got him a glass of water while Mr. Samson was in here looking this stuff up on the computer. When Dr. Hollister went upstairs to get Abby, Mr. Samson called his wife in here to look at these websites. Afraid the doctor would discover what they found out, they closed the websites and went upstairs."

Steve began pacing the floor. "For some reason, Dr. Hollister must have pulled out his gun and forced them to leave their phones on Abby's bed. Then, using their daughter as a hostage, he told them to get in their car and follow him. He would take Abby with him in his SUV."

Tyrone nodded slowly. "And without their cell phones, they couldn't call for help. And if they tried to pull over anywhere, they'd lose Abby."

"Exactly," Steve said.

Matt looked confused. "But where would he take them?"

Tyrone looked solemn. "I don't know, but we'd better figure that out. If that man hurts any one of them…" His voice trailed off and his hands clenched into fists.

"Hello?" A faint female voice sounded in the room.

Steve's eyes grew wide. "Oh, man. Alysha!" He put Tyrone's phone up to his face. "Alysha! I am so sorry. I forgot I had you on the phone."

"That's okay. I got to hear everything that was going on. Listen, you should check all their phones, especially Abby's."

Steve frowned. "Check for what?"

"If they were smart, and by 'they' I really mean Abby, because adults are completely clueless when it comes to technology, they might've recorded the conversation. Check the camera and see if any of them pressed record."

Steve told everyone Alysha's plan, then the three kids each grabbed a phone.

"This one's locked," Matt said and started pushing buttons. "Any idea what the number code might be?"

Steve held up the phone in his hand. "This one is locked, too."

"Bingo!" Jenny said triumphantly. "This one, which by the way has to be Abby's unless one of her parents has a mad love for Hello Kitty. Anyway, this one is not only unlocked, but she totally did hit record. It looks like the video is about five minutes long."

"Play it," Matt said, excitement in his voice.

Jenny fumbled with the phone. "Hold on. Let me turn up the volume."

She pressed play. The group crowded around to see the video. The screen showed nothing but the ceiling.

"Now what?" Mr. Samson's deep voice sounded over the phone's speaker.

"Yeah," Abby said. "We put our phones down. Will you leave us alone?"

Dr. Hollister's laugh filled the room. Steve noticed Tyrone's fists clench again. He would not want to be in the doctor's shoes when Tyrone got a hold of him.

"I'm afraid that is no longer possible."

"Why would you do this?" Mrs. Samson said. "I don't understand. Why put Abby through all this? And what about Dr. Rollings? Is he a part of this scheme, too?"

Mr. Samson chimed in. "Is he the one that gave you this idea? Are you in on this together?"

Dr. Hollister gave a short laugh. "That simpleton? Please. Don't you get it? *I* was the thief. When the clients became suspicious, I framed him and convinced the board to fire him. It was so easy.

No one ever suspected. Just as no one suspected about Abby."

"But why?" Mrs. Samson asked. "You were going to have us check her into a mental institution."

"With Dr. Rollings, yes. But only for the psych exams. Honestly, he would have found nothing wrong with her and chalked this whole thing up to a wild imagination. Abby would have been home in a few days. But now, I'm afraid things will have to be different."

"What are you planning to do with us?" Mrs. Samson sounded nervous.

The doctor sighed. "I'll have to keep you out of the way for a while, until I can disappear. Let's go."

"Wait." Mr. Samson said. "Abby doesn't need to be a part of this. Take us."

"Not a chance. That girl is much smarter than you give her credit for. One of the things I can tell you from our sessions, you need to work on communicating better with your daughter. Now, move!"

"Can I take my bear?" Abby's gentle voice sounded.

"Sure."

Abby's face appeared for a moment on the screen as she reached over the phone to grab her bear. She looked down at the camera and mouthed the words, "Help us." Then she disappeared.

"And just in case you get any crazy ideas," the doctor's voice started to fade, "just remember I've…"

The voice trailed off. Steve assumed the Samsons and their abductor left the room. The group waited quietly to see if anything else happened on the video. At the end of five minutes, the video stopped.

Jenny put the phone down. "What are we gonna do?"

"The only logical thing we can do," Steve said. "Go rescue them."

12 TRAPPED!

Steve watched the others stare at him on disbelief.

"Rescue them?" Matt repeated. "How? We don't even know where he took them."

"I think we do," Steve said. "Dr. Hollister wasn't expecting the Samsons to discover his secret. Their confronting him forced him to step up his time schedule. Remember what he said at the cabin? He planned to be out of the country tomorrow. Now that he has witnesses, he's going to need to get out as soon as possible. That means, he needs to take the Samsons somewhere they'll be out of sight, the one place he knows is isolated, with no neighbors, where he can—"

"The cabin!" Jenny interrupted.

Steve nodded. "Exactly."

Tyrone grabbed his cell out of Steve's hands.

"Sorry, Alysha, but I need my phone right now. We'll call you back." He hung up and began dialing. "I'm calling the cops on this one."

"I thought you had to wait twenty-four hours," Matt said.

"Not when I've got this video. Hello?" He spoke into the phone. "Yeah, put me through to Detective Carter. Tell him it's Tyrone Washington."

Within fifteen minutes, four police cars arrived at the Samson house. Tyrone had explained everything to the detective who dispatched patrol cars to the residence to view the tape and get directions for the cabin. The group told the police of their desire to go with them. The officers agreed to allow Tyrone to accompany them, but not the Decoders.

"Sorry, kids," the policeman said. "We can't take children to a potentially dangerous situation."

Frustrated, the three twelve-year-olds agreed to wait at Abby's house.

After the motorcade left, Jenny plopped on a couch and crossed her arms. "This is like so annoying! I can't believe we have to stay here while all the action is going on without us."

Matt sat on the sofa next to her. "I know what you mean. But at least, for the first time since we started solving mysteries, the police are actually going to be the ones to catch the bad guy."

"Perhaps," Steve said.

"Huh?" Matt said, looking confused.

Jenny uncrossed her arms. "What do you mean, 'perhaps'?"

Steve pointed at his watch. "It's almost eleven-thirty. Do you remember what time Dr. Hollister told us he was going to be dropping off Abby?"

"He said around ten," Matt answered.

Steve began pacing around the room. "Which means, he probably came by here around nine o'clock or so."

Jenny sat up straight. "I get it. That video was shot like way over two hours ago."

"Exactly. If the doctor left here with the Samsons a couple hours ago to take them to the cabin, then he would have arrived there between ten-thirty and eleven."

Matt glanced at his own watch. "And at this rate, the police won't even get to the cabin till twelve-thirty. The doc will be long gone."

Steve nodded. "The good news is that the police will rescue the Samsons. My guess is they'll be handcuffed to the table, just like we were."

Jenny giggled and leaned forward. "I wonder what doc thought when he opened the cabin door and we were gone. He probably totally freaked out."

Matt held up his hand. "Hold on. You said the good news is that the Samsons would be rescued. I'm guessing the bad news is that the doctor will have gotten away."

Steve stopped pacing. "Unless *we* catch him."

"Catch him?" Matt repeated.

"How?" Jenny asked.

Steve resumed pacing. "The Samsons confronting him forced him to speed up his time table. I believe seeing us gone has now made him panic. He's going to want to get out of here as quickly as possible before we can identify him to the authorities."

"You think he'll make a break for it?" Matt asked.

Steve stopped and faced him. "I'm sure of it."

Jenny jumped up. "Then what are we waiting for? Let's get to the airport!"

Matt shook his head. "How are we supposed to get there? We don't even have our bikes."

Steve headed toward the kitchen. "I saw a landline over here. Let's call Tyrone and tell him our theory. He can tell the police and they can call it in and have cops sent to the airport."

Jenny followed her friend closely. "What about us?"

Steve picked up the phone and began dialing. "I'm not sure. The officers made it clear they don't want us anywhere near the action. Hello? Tyrone?" Steve explained their theory to their friend who passed the information on to the policemen in the car.

"And Tyrone," Steve added. "We'd like to go

to the airport, too. It's a big place with lots of people. I think we'd be really helpful. Think you can find us a ride?"

There was a pause, then Tyrone spoke. "Yeah, all right. No problem. I'll take care of it." He hung up.

"What'd he say?" Matt asked.

Steve put down the phone. "He said he'd take care of it. I'm guessing he didn't want the cops in the car to hear he was sending us a ride."

Jenny headed for the front door. "We should wait outside, so we don't waste any time."

The boys agreed and the three of them rushed out to the front porch.

After several minutes, Jenny began tapping her foot. "What if he's already there? He could be boarding a plane right now."

Steve shook his head. "I think we're good, as long as our ride gets here soon. Remember, Dr. Hollister was planning on skipping town tomorrow. Once he dropped the Samson family off at the cabin, he would've had to go get the jewels, wherever he's been stashing them." He paused and bit his lip. "Unless, he hid the stolen jewels in his SUV."

Matt looked at his watch. "Either way, we're cutting it pretty close. He's got a big head start on us."

Just then, a bright yellow taxi pulled into the

driveway. The kids ran up to it and climbed in the back seat. The driver turned around, smiling. "Hey, now. I remember you three. Seems to me, we made this same airport run about two weeks ago."

The kids all laughed, remembering Tyrone's friend from their first mystery.

Steve chuckled. "I guess you could say this is sort of a déjà vu thing."

The cab pulled onto the main road. "Ty said you three were in a pretty big hurry. Chasing down another criminal, eh?"

"Another jewel thief," Jenny said.

"Well, make sure your seat belts are fastened, 'cause this cab's on a mission."

In fifteen minutes, the taxi pulled up to the airport terminal.

"How much do we owe you?" Steve asked.

The man shook his head. "Ty's friends are my friends. Besides," he paused and grinned, "I'll get some of Ty's food out of this. Don't you worry."

The kids thanked the cabbie and rushed into the terminal. Just before entering the building, Steve noticed several parked police cars. The cops were here someplace, but unless they accessed the doctor's police record on the way there, they didn't know what the doctor looked like. The Decoders did. "Let's split up," he said finally. "We'll cover more ground that way."

"But we don't have phones this time," Matt

protested. "Or our flashlights. How will we let each other know if we find him?"

"We don't have to let each other know," Steve said. "We need to let the cops know. If you spot him, look for a policeman or security guard and tell them."

The others agreed and the threesome split up. Steve went left, being sure to look at every single person walking by. The last time they were in the airport looking for a suspect, the man out-smarted them by dressing as a woman and walking right by them. Not this time. Steve would not be fooled again. If Dr. Hollister was here, they would find him, in disguise or not.

Because of the amount of people in the airport, his search went slowly. Twenty minutes later he reached the end of the terminal and turned around. Another twenty minutes and he ran into Matt and Jenny, who also turned up empty handed.

"Now what?" Matt asked.

"We keep looking," Steve answered.

Jenny nodded. "Right. Last time, we didn't find the bad guys until the second time around."

They split up again. This time, Steve decided to do a quick investigation outside. He gazed down the sidewalk in both directions as far as he could see. The doctor wasn't there. But parked not too far from him, sat a bus. The driver glanced at her watch as though waiting for her departure time.

Steve glanced at the sign. It was the intra-terminal shuttle. This bus connected the airport to the bus/train depot a few miles away. Steve bit his lip in thought. If the doctor had indeed arrived at the airport, he may have seen the police cars and panicked. But no cops were waiting at the train station. Steve had to get on that shuttle.

He looked around frantically and pulled down a nearby flyer advertising a music concert. He ripped off the tape, cut it into four small strips, attached them onto the bus stop sign in the form of a "D," then climbed into the shuttle just before it pulled away. Not seeing the doctor on board, Steve settled into a seat near the front, hoping his friends would find the clue he left them.

Jenny studied the inside of the restroom. She waited until the last person left, did a quick sweep to make sure the doctor wasn't hiding out, and then exited. After their last pursuit at the airport, she wasn't taking any chances, every nook and cranny would be checked. She soon spotted Matt looking in a broom closet.

"Anything?" she asked as she joined him.

He shook his head and closed the door. "How about you?"

She also shook her head. "Have you seen Steve?"

"Not yet. But I have seen about ten cops.

They're all over the place. If that dude is here, he's crazy. They'll catch him for sure."

She nodded, still keeping her eyes on the lookout. "I was thinking the same thing. Let's find Steve. We've got to come up with a new plan."

Matt agreed and the two of them began scouring the terminal looking for their friend. After almost a half hour, Jenny raised her hands in the air in exasperation. "Where in the world is he? Ugh! It is so frustrating not having a phone."

Matt pointed to an information booth. "Let's page him."

She smiled, relieved. "That's a good idea."

They walked over and spoke to the woman behind the desk who nodded.

Soon her voice sounded over the airport intercom. "Paging Steve Kemp. Please meet your party at the information booth. Steve Kemp. Your party is waiting at the information booth."

The two kids thanked the woman and waited. Five minutes later, they had the woman page him again. After another couple of minutes, Jenny began biting her thumb nail. "Where is he?"

Matt shook his head slowly. "I have a bad feeling about this."

The two kids looked at each other, worried.

Steve jumped off the bus and ran into the terminal. Center Union Station, called CU Station by locals, was split in two: the upstairs was a train station, with long-distance passenger trains and local commuter trains; the lower floor was a bus station, with transfer buses from all over the city. If the jewel thief was here, he could be anywhere.

The boy began his search up at the train platform. There were far fewer people there than the airport, so the search was much quicker. Not finding the doctor anywhere, he moved his investigation to the lower level.

That floor held significantly more people, all of whom seemed to be in a hurry. It was also incredibly loud. The train sounds from above mixed with the running buses and horns from downstairs made hearing anything else almost impossible. People standing next to each other were practically yelling to make themselves heard.

Steve wandered through the crowd, pushed around several times by people in a hurry to catch their bus. If the doctor was here, finding him was going to be nearly impossible. He gritted his teeth. Nearly impossible was not impossible. He just needed to focus. Steve saw a shoeshine stand sitting vacant and dodged between people to make his way over to it. Climbing up on one of the chairs, he now stood about two or three feet above the crowd. He searched frantically and then, he saw him! Or at least, someone that looked like him. The man was walking away from the terminal, toward the buses.

Steve jumped down and began shoving his way through the masses. After apologizing a million times for running into people, he finally made it to the parked buses. The man had disappeared. And from his height, Steve couldn't see over the crowd. He ran back and forth, trying to peer inside the large vehicles, but there was simply too much activity. Frustrated, he made his way back through the mob toward the building.

Abruptly, strong hands grabbed his shoulders from behind, and Steve found himself getting pulled inside a bathroom. The door closed behind him and the strong arms pushed him down to the ground. Steve looked up and saw Dr. Hollister standing in front of him, his gun drawn.

"I don't know how you escaped from the cabin, but I will not have you following me here." He grabbed Steve's right arm and squeezed one side of a pair of handcuffs on his wrist so hard that Steve winced. The other side of the handcuffs were tightened around the handicap bar on the wall. Next, the doctor put handcuffs on each of the boy's ankles, binding them together.

"You won't get away this time," Steve said. "The police are onto you."

The man laughed. "I told you I had a contingency plan, didn't I?" He took a handkerchief out of his pocket and put it in Steve's mouth. As the doctor tied the gag, Steve noticed a ticket sticking out of his pocket. It was a bus ticket to San Francisco. He could only make out the first digit of the time: 3. He was leaving at three-something on a bus for San Francisco.

Steve tried to tell him again that he wasn't going to get away with this and that the police would find him before he left the station, but with the gag in his mouth, nothing made sense.

Dr. Hollister smiled. "Scream all you want. With all that noise out there, no one will hear you." He held up a key. "Borrowed this from a member of the cleaning crew. You'll be locked up in here for quite a while. But even I have to admit, you are pretty clever. So, to make sure you cause me no further problems, I have this." He pulled a small vile from his pocket. "I have my own special blend of nitrous oxide. I use it sometimes in my sessions to calm the nerves of some of my more…erratic patients."

The slender man shook the vial. "I'm sure you're familiar with laughing gas. I understand dentists use it quite frequently with children. Well, my formula is slightly different. Oh, you get the same light-headedness as regular laughing gas, but mine actually puts you to sleep. What better way to keep you out of my way than having you chained to the wall, in lullaby-land. By the time the custodians discover you, I will be long gone, on my flight to freedom." He opened the door. "Good-bye, kid.

Sweet dreams." He smashed the vial on the ground and quickly closed the door.

Steve held his breath as he heard the lock turn. Stretching as far as he could with his free arm, he tried desperately to reach the doorknob but did not come close. He banged on the wall for a few seconds then stopped, remembering there was a closet next door to him and nobody would hear him. Finally, he exhaled and drew a quick breath in. He hopped to the back of the restroom and banged on the wall there. His beatings made very little noise. Even if there was a walkway behind the restroom, the chances of someone hearing him were almost zero.

As he inhaled his next breath, he detected the sweet smell of the laughing gas. He looked at his watch and leaned against the wall. It was two-fifteen. The police must have found the cabin and rescued the Samsons by now. Tyrone would've wanted to head over to the airport immediately afterwards. By Steve's guess, Tyrone would be arriving there any minute. He'd eventually run into Matt and Jenny, who were probably trying to figure out where Steve had gone.

They'd all three look around the airport. When they couldn't find him, they'd look outside. Then, while studying every inch of the outside décor, they'd see the "D" tape on the intra-terminal sign. They'd hop on the bus, arrive here, and resume their search. After a thorough investigation, they'd notice the locked bathroom, have a custodian open it, and he'd be rescued.

Steve sighed again. And then, pigs would fly. He giggled. Flying pigs. He laughed out loud, then shook his head to clear it. This was hopeless. He was stuck in here until the custodians came to clean. Although he would be saved, the doctor would be gone. And all the jewels with him. He closed his eyes and thought of his friends. *Please find me*. His eyelids started feeling heavy and his body sank to the floor. *You must find me.*

13 A STRANGE VIBE

Matt shook his head. "This is crazy. Steve has to be around here someplace. He wouldn't have left without telling us."

"But how could he tell us?" Jenny pointed out. "We don't have our cells."

Matt shuffled his feet. "Oh, man! What if he saw the doc and tried following him and the dude pulled his gun on him?"

Jenny frowned and made a circle with her arm. "In this crowded airport?"

"It wouldn't be that hard. Think about it. In movies, they always show some thug holding a gun inside a newspaper or something. Dr. Hollister could easily have done that."

"Matt! Jenny!" A voice called out from the crowd.

The two kids whirled around.

Tyrone ran up to them. "What's happening? Did you guys find the doctor?"

Matt shook his head. "Nope. And now, we can't find Steve, either."

Tyrone's eyebrows shot up. "What? What happened?"

Matt and Jenny took turns telling their friend about their experience since arriving at the airport.

The tall man shook his head. "This is not good."

"How about the Samsons?" Jenny asked. "Did you find them?"

He nodded. "Yep. They were handcuffed to the table, just like you all said they'd be."

"And they're all okay?" Matt asked, concerned.

"Every one of them. Denise said Dr. Hollister was really upset when they walked into the cabin. He started mumbling something about a contingency plan. I didn't tell them about you three being tied up in there. No sense in worrying them."

"Did they ask you how you knew to look for them in that cabin?" Jenny asked.

"Yeah. I told them I hired a team of PIs called The Decoders to solve this mystery. It was these private investigators who discovered the cabin and figured out that's where Dr. Hollister would've taken them."

Jenny laughed. "The funny thing is, it's all true."

Matt pushed his hair out of his eyes and grinned. "Yeah, I'm not sure most PIs discover the bad guy's hiding spot by getting themselves kidnapped."

"Speaking of which," Tyrone's voice turned solemn, "we need to find Steve. I'm not liking his disappearance."

"That makes two of us," Jenny said.

"Make that three," Matt added.

The trio split up. While Jenny searched one side of the terminal, Matt scoured the other. Tyrone stayed in the middle to keep an eye on everything, just in case. When their search came up empty, they regrouped to decide on a new course of action.

"Maybe Steve followed him through security," Matt suggested.

Jenny frowned. "Then he would've needed to buy a ticket. They don't let you through unless you've already got one."

"He might have snuck through somehow. Remember that story in the news about that seven-year-old that made it all the way across the country by telling everyone some story about his parents leaving him in the restroom? Steve could've made up some crazy story like that."

Tyrone shrugged. "It's worth a shot. I'll go ask security. Either of you got a picture of him?"

Jenny nodded. "Yeah, I do, on my...ugh! I seriously hate not having my cell. So, then, no, I don't have a picture of him. Or anybody else, for that matter."

"That's all right. You all wait here."

After Tyrone left, Matt and Jenny decided to check outside. They looked up and down the sidewalk, but found nothing.

Without warning, Jenny grabbed her friend's arm. "Matt, look!" She rushed forward, without easing her grip on him. She pointed to the intra-terminal bus stop sign. "Check it out."

Matt squinted his eyes, then his eyebrows shot up in surprise. "No way. It's the D signal."

"Go get Tyrone. We know where Steve went."

Matt followed Jenny and Tyrone out of a cab at Central Union Station. They had informed the police back at the airport about their theory, then decided to hop a taxi to the terminal on their own.

Matt took a quick scan of the area and couldn't believe how many people were there.

Tyrone motioned to the two different levels of the terminal. "How are we gonna play this?"

Jenny pointed to the upstairs. "I'll take the top floor and Matt, you take the bottom. Tyrone, you stay near the center escalators. That way if either of us misses Steve, you'll see him."

They all agreed and the two kids left to continue the hunt for their missing friend.

Matt began his search of the bus terminal. So

many people were rushing around that he found himself constantly dodging arms and apologizing for stepping on toes. If Steve was mixed into this crowd, he would be hard to see. Before long, he found vacant shoeshine chairs and climbed on top of them. Although the elevated level made seeing the masses easier, trying to see every single person walking by was impossible.

As he left to make his way toward the escalator, a strange sensation came over him. It was the same feeling Matt got when he was about to fail a test. He shook his head, but it wouldn't leave.

Matt waved at Tyrone as he approached. "Anything?"

Tyrone shook his head. "No. You?"

Just then, Jenny waved from the upper floor, motioning that she was coming down.

"See anything?" Matt asked as she joined them.

She shook her head. "No, but I had the weirdest feeling while I was up there."

Matt perked up. "Like what?"

She shrugged. "I don't know. It was like I wasn't supposed to be there. I can't explain it."

"I think I know what you mean." Matt then related his own experience. "Isn't that weird?"

Jenny crossed her arms and rubbed them. "More like super creepy. What are the chances of both of us having these strange feelings here at the station?"

Tyrone scratched his chin. "Hold up. Jenny, you got those strange feelings when you went upstairs. Did they go away when you came down here?"

She paused before answering. "Yeah. I didn't even think of that. They're gone now."

Tyrone nodded. "And Matt. You said you didn't get that sensation until you started heading back here. Do you still have it?"

Matt thought for a moment. "Yeah, actually. It's like something bad is about to happen."

"But you didn't feel it when you were over by the buses?" Tyrone said.

The boy scrunched his forehead in thought. "Nope. I didn't notice it till I was walking back here."

Tyrone began walking toward the bus depot. "Come on."

The two kids looked at each other briefly, then rushed to catch up to their friend.

"Where are we going?" Jenny asked.

"I believe Steve is somewhere near the buses. Somehow, he's sending you guys a vibe."

"A vibe?" Matt repeated, trying not to sound as confused as he felt.

"Didn't you all say Steve had some kind of psychic connection with that sapphire in the cave?" He was referring to a situation that occurred on their first case, The Magic Sapphire.

Matt shrugged. "Yeah, dude, but that sapphire's in a museum miles away from here. What does it have to do with what's going on now?"

Tyrone stopped. "Where were you when you decided to return to the escalator?"

Matt pointed. "Over there."

Tyrone resumed walking, heading in the direction Matt indicated. "I know this sounds crazy, but it's possible Steve's got a psychic connection to you two as well."

"Seriously?" Matt said.

"What do you mean?" Jenny asked.

"All I'm saying is that if Steve is in trouble down here, it could be that you two picked up on it. That's why Jenny felt like she shouldn't be upstairs and why Matt began feeling uncomfortable when he started to leave here."

He stopped by the empty shoeshine chairs.

"This is it," Matt said. "I was standing on one of these chairs looking around when I decided to head back to the escalator. That's when that weird feeling hit me."

Jenny looked around. 'So, if Tyrone's right, Steve must be around here somewhere."

"But where?" Matt said.

"How about we walk around?" Tyrone suggested. "Let's see what we find."

The trio began making their way toward the buses. With so many people, it was difficult to stick together, and it didn't take long for Matt to become separated from the others. It could be that the doctor and Steve were on board a bus. As he neared the buses, that same strange feeling returned. He looked back toward the terminal building. Something told him Steve was behind him, somewhere near the shoeshine stand.

He walked back toward the wall and ran into Jenny. "Hey," he said. "I tried going over toward the buses but that same weird feeling came back again."

She nodded. "Me, too. Steve has to be around here someplace. But where?"

Tyrone walked up. "Anything?"

They explained their renewed sensations of uneasiness and how they intensified as they walked away from the building.

"All right, we'll keep our search close to the building." The man looked around. "Any idea which way to go?"

Matt studied the wall. He felt like there was something right in front of him that he was missing. But what?

"Hey," Jenny's voice interrupted his thoughts. "This bathroom. It's been occupied since we first got here."

Matt shrugged. "It's a busy bus station. I'm sure their bathrooms are always full."

Jenny shook her head. "Not the big handicap

ones like this. It's not like there's a line waiting for it."

Tyrone banged on the restroom door. "Hello? Anybody in there?"

No response.

"Dude," Matt said nervously, "they might be kinda embarrassed."

Tyrone pounded again. "Hey, you okay in there? You need me to get some help?" He tried the doorknob, but it was locked.

"I'll go find a custodian. You two keep your eyes on it in case someone comes out."

After Tyrone left, Jenny turned to Matt. "Okay, you watch the door, and I'll focus on the crowd." She walked a little ways into the masses.

Matt grunted and turned his body to face the door. Staking out a bathroom felt totally weird and uncomfortable. But at the same time, he felt like they were on the right track.

He heard Jenny yell out. "It's the doctor! I'm going after him."

"Jenny, wait!" Matt turned around, but couldn't see her amidst all the people. Deciding that she was in more pressing danger than Steve in a locked bathroom, Matt took off running into the crowd. Then he heard it. A gunshot!

Matt's heart stopped beating and the blood drained from his face. Jenny! He pushed his way forward as people were screaming and running for cover. He made it to the center of the dispersing crowd and stopped short in his tracks. There, in front of him, stood Dr. Hollister with a gun held to the back of Jenny's head.

"Let her go!" Matt said, the blood rising to his head. He balled his fists and took a step forward. The doctor moved the barrel of the gun to her temple. Matt stopped.

"Not another step."'

"Okay, doc," Matt said. "But please, let her go."

Dr. Hollister gave a short laugh. "Let her go? She's my only ticket out of here now."

Matt noticed policemen moving in, directing the crowd to back away.

"Dr. Hollister," Tyrone's voice sounded through the crowd before he appeared in-between two policemen. "It's over, man. The Samsons have been rescued from the cabin. They told the police about all the jewels you stole from them and how you hypnotized Abby to help you." As he spoke, additional policeman filled in the area. "You don't want to make this any worse than it already is. Let the girl go."

The doctor backed up a step, taking Jenny with him. "There's a plane waiting for me in San Francisco. There's no way I'm missing that flight. So, here's the deal. The girl comes with me. Once I'm one the plane, I'll let her go."

"No way." Matt took a step forward. "If you're taking anyone, you're taking me."

"No, you'll take me." Tyrone stepped forward.

"I said I'm going." Matt took another step forward.

Tyrone also moved forward. "And I said I'm going."

As the doctor looked between the boy and the man, he appeared a bit disoriented. Jenny took advantage and, with all her might, elbowed him as hard as she could in the stomach, weakening his grip on her. She pulled free and ran as fast as she could straight to Matt who grabbed her arms and pulled her behind a nearby policeman.

The moment Jenny was free from the doctor's grip, Tyrone lunged at him, knocking the man to the ground and the gun out of his hand. As the doctor attempted to get up, Tyrone gave him a sharp right hook to the jaw that sent him sprawling to the ground. "That was for Abby."

The police swarmed the doctor, placing his wrists in handcuffs. Tyrone walked over to the two kids. "You okay? he asked Jenny.

She nodded, clinging to Matt's arm. "Yeah."

Matt grinned. "Dude, that was some punch you gave him. Man, am I jealous."

Tyrone smiled. "Yeah, I can't lie. It felt pretty good, especially after what he's put you all through."

"Oh my gosh," Jenny said. "Steve!"

They rushed back to the restroom and Tyrone found a custodian. When they opened the door, Steve was on the ground half asleep.

"Steve!" Matt rushed up to him.

The sleepy boy looked up and grinned. "Hi, Matt. What are you doing here?"

Jenny pulled a paperclip out of her jeans pocket and worked on the handcuffs binding his ankles. "I got this."

"Steve," Tyrone said as he examined the boy's eyes. "You okay?"

Steve chuckled. "Yeah. The doctor smashed a vial of laughing gas in here. Isn't that funny? Get it? Laughing gas? Funny?" He burst out laughing.

Once Jenny undid the handcuff on his wrist, she and Matt lifted Steve up and put his arms around their shoulders to help him walk. They made it out of the bathroom and Steve saw all the police activity. His eyes widened and he stopped walking. "Hey, I just remembered. The doctor. He's going to San Francisco. I saw his ticket."

"Don't worry, Steve," Tyrone said. "We got him."

Steve looked confused. "You went to San Francisco? How come you didn't take me?"

Jenny laughed. "We didn't go to San Francisco. We caught him here, in the bus station."

His eyes widened. "Really? You got him?"

171

"Yeah," Matt added enthusiastically. "You should've seen it. Tyrone gave him a punch that sent him flying."

Steve giggled. "Whoa. What kind of punch makes you fly? Is that like a Hawaiian punch or something? Sort of a flywaiian punch?" He laughed hysterically.

Matt shook his head. "Oh, brother."

"Um, Tyrone," Jenny said. "How long is he gonna be like this?"

"Now that he's not breathing in the laughing gas anymore, it should wear off in like a half-hour."

Matt looked at Tyrone in distress. "I don't know if I can handle this for a half-hour."

"Matt," Steve said solemnly. "You can handle anything. I mean *anything*. After all, you're Matt Peterson. You're the bravest guy I know. Hey, your last name is Peterson, like Son of Peter, but your dad's name isn't Peter. Isn't that weird?" He started laughing again.

Matt groaned. "Seriously? A half-hour of this?"

14 RECANTING THE ADVENTURE

The next night, Steve joined Matt, Jenny, and Alysha at Tyrone's Diner for a big, end-of-the-mystery dinner.

"How are you feeling now?" Alysha's asked Steve, as she reached over and took another roll from the bread basket.

He swallowed the large bite of pot roast in his mouth. "Much better now, thanks. It's nice to be able to think clearly without my head being all fuzzy."

Matt grinned as he poured a puddle of Ranch dressing onto his plate. "It was pretty funny, though. You laughed at everything."

Jenny took a sip from her soda. "Literally, everything. You even laughed at Matt's jokes, so you *know* you were totally out of your mind."

Matt frowned. "Hey, now. I can be funny."

"Yeah," Jenny said, a twinkle in her eye. "Funny looking."

Matt made a face at her, then dunked the chicken finger in his hand into the pool of Ranch and stuffed it in his mouth.

Tyrone leaned back. "I'm just glad you all are okay."

"How's Abby doing?" Jenny asked.

"She's good. Her parents are taking a couple of days off and the three of them are going on a vacation."

Steve nodded. "Excellent. They deserve it."

Alysha put her fork down and interlocked her fingers. "Okay, I know you guys explained this to me when you got home last night, but I'm still a little confused on the details of what exactly Dr. Hollister was doing. Think you could walk me through it again? I'd like to make some notes for my next Decoders article."

A whiz with words, Alysha often wrote articles for the local newspaper, including articles about the mysterious detectives known as the Decoders and their latest mysteries. She pulled out a tablet from her purse. "Okay, ready when you are."

Tyrone poured more water into his glass. "It all started when my sister Denise would find Abby sleeping in strange places around the house. She figured that Abby was sleepwalking and decided to get her some help."

"That's when they called Dr. Hollister," Jenny added.

"Exactly," he continued. "The doctor came recommended by a friend of theirs, so they didn't even bother checking into him. At first, he was actually treating her and she started getting better. But then, once he began noticing the jewelry my sister would wear to the sessions, he began formulating a plan. He claimed that in order to progress with the therapy, they would need to move the sessions to her home."

Matt slurped his chocolate shake. "Basically, he wanted to case the house."

"Once he got a good layout of the place," Steve took over, "he started hypnosis sessions with Abby. The first time she was under, he programmed a ringtone into her phone and hypnotized her to open the window in her bedroom and the bathroom. Then, that night, he made his practice run. He called her on the phone using his special ringtone. She answered the phone and immediately opened the windows, then crawled back into bed and went back to sleep."

"He didn't steal anything that night?" Alysha asked.

"No," Steve answered. "He just wanted to see if Abby was reacting to the hypnosis. After that, during each session, he would program Abby to open the windows, steal a specific jewelry piece, then crawl back into bed. He would then send his trained bat in through the open window in the restroom, retrieve the jewelry, and fly out the bedroom window."

Alysha frowned. "I thought Abby would wake up in strange places again. Didn't you guys find her by the pool?"

Steve nodded. "After a few nights of success, Dr. Hollister became afraid that the Samsons would decide Abby didn't need his services anymore. That's when he started having her go back to sleep at various places. The pool was a great one for him. Her parents were freaked out that she could've drowned in her sleep."

Jenny leaned back and crossed her arms. "He was giving himself job security. As long as Abby kept sleepwalking, her parents wouldn't fire him."

Steve continued the story. "But then, Abby decided to video tape herself. On her camera, she filmed herself getting up, opening the window in her bedroom, then disappear into the bathroom. Moments later, a bat flew out of the bathroom."

Tyrone took over. "And Abby, having the wild imagination that she does, believed she was turning into a vampire bat. That's when she called me and asked me for help. She was afraid that her parents would send her to a funny farm if she told them she was a vampire."

"And that's when Tyrone called us." Matt

stuffed the last French fry on his plate into his mouth.

Ringing interrupted their conversation. Jenny pulled a cell phone out of her pocket. She looked at the caller, hit silent, then returned it to her pocket.

"Is that your new cell?" Alysha asked.

"Yeah. Dad said if I lose this one, I have to pay for the next one out of my own pocket."

Steve pushed his empty plate forward. "My parents said the same thing." He pulled his phone out. "Although, I actually like this one better than the last one I had. Hopefully, it'll be around for a while."

"That is a nice phone," Alysha commented, "How about you, Matt? Did you get a new phone, too?"

Jenny burst out laughing. "Yeah, Matt. Show Alysha your new phone."

Matt sighed and pulled out his new phone. "My mom was so mad."

"How many cell phones did you say you've lost?" Tyrone asked.

"Five. Yeah, Mom was not about to buy me another one. So, this is her old cell from like 2005. No internet, no texting, just phone calls."

"Wow," Jenny looked awed. "Can I see that? It's so retro. Does it even have a camera?"

He shook his head and handed the phone over to his friend. "It's got nothing. Mom says if I can keep this one around until Christmas, she might buy me a new one. So, no matter what mysteries we find ourselves wrapped up in for the next six months, I cannot lose this phone."

"Maybe I can help with that," Tyrone said. "I've got a surprise for the three of you."

Matt's face lit up. "Is it a pie?"

Tyrone laughed. "Not exactly. I'll be right back."

Jenny watched him disappear into the kitchen, then turned to face her friend. "A pie? Seriously, Matt, do you ever think about anything besides food?"

"Hey," he said defensively, "I like pie. Everybody likes pie. Or, maybe, he's bringing out a cake. I like cake, too."

Tyrone reappeared carrying three medium-sized gift bags. He handed one to each of the Decoders.

"What's this for?" Steve asked.

"It's your payment. I did hire you, remember?"

Steve, Matt, and Jenny all three tried to hand back the bags.

Steve shook his head. "No way. You're our friend."

"You've helped us out a gazillion times before," Matt added.

Jenny nodded. "Yeah, if anything, we owe you for all the help you've given us."

Tyrone smiled. "These are non-refundable. Besides, you three seriously saved my niece's life, not to mention my sister's fortune. Come on. Open them up."

The three friends looked at each other and grinned. They simultaneously grabbed their bags and pulled out their presents.

"Are these…" Jenny's voice trailed off.

Tyrone pointed to the box in her hand. "They're pre-paid cell phones. Unlimited calls, texts, and data for six months. After that, you're on your own."

Jenny jumped up and hugged him. "Thank you so much. These are amazing."

He laughed. "Now, you all can leave your regular phones at home when you go out chasing bad guys. That way, if they get lost or crushed, Matt's mom won't have to bury him in the backyard."

Matt grinned. "Seriously, dude. These are the best gifts ever."

"Better than pie?"

Everyone laughed. "Yeah," Matt said. "Even better than pie."

Just then, a waitress came over carrying a hot apple pie. "Well, that's good," Tyrone said. "But, I've got pie, too."

Steve watched Matt's expression go from happy to uncontrollably excited. As everyone thanked Tyrone and began diving into their dessert, Steve wondered what the future of the Decoders would hold. But, no matter what mystery waited for them next, one thing was for sure: Steve was tired of the bad guys always having the advantage.

Tomorrow, they start taking self-defense classes.

BOOKS BY ALBA ARANGO

The Decoders Series

The Magic Sapphire

The Lady Ghost

The Sleepwalking Vampire

The Mysterious Music Box

The Statue of Anubis

The Miner's Gold

The JJ Bennett: Junior Spy Series

Problems in Prague

Jeopardy in Geneva

Bedlam in Berlin

Danger in Dublin

Last Stand in London

ABOUT THE AUTHOR

Alba Arango is the author of the Decoders series as well as the JJ Bennett: Junior Spy series. She lives in Las Vegas, Nevada, where she is a retired high school teacher turned full-time author. She loves coffee and chocolate (especially together...white chocolate mocha is the best!).

To learn more about Alba, visit her website at AlbaArango.com.

Instagram @AlbaArango.007

Twitter @AlbaArango007

Facebook: Alba Arango Author Page